THE DEAD GIRL

Breakdown

DEBRA WEBB

PINK
HOUSE
PRESS

Pink House Press, Madison, Alabama

First Edition October 2018

THE DEAD GIRL

Debra Webb

A Novel

CHAPTER ONE

Thursday, October 4

Two years.

Apparently that was to be the extent of Laney Holt's reprieve in paradise.

Laney stared at the dead girl on the floor. How the hell did a beautiful young woman who had the perfect life in the perfect town get herself murdered?

Pushing to her feet, Laney turned to the uniform standing by. "Find McCabe."

"Yes, ma'am."

Officer Seth Trask, the first on the scene, hustled out of the room. Their chief of police hadn't answered his phone when Laney called him. Knowing his bad habits better than she cared to, it was a relatively simple matter to guess that he had likely over indulged last night. She hadn't broached the subject with him, but in the course of working together for the past two years she couldn't help noticing Shutter Lake's chief of police had a deep and serious relationship with alcohol.

Laney listened for the front door to close behind Trask. When she heard the telltale sound of wood against wood her gaze settled on the victim once more. "Shit."

The coffee she'd gulped down on the drive from Main Street to Olive Tree Lane churned in her belly. Typically she grabbed a bagel with her coffee, but this morning her cell had buzzed with the call about a body before she'd made up her mind whether she wanted a blueberry or a poppy seed bagel. Cream cheese or honey? Instead of a leisurely morning discussing any homeless folks who had taken up residence at the century old mine outside of town, she was analyzing the kind of scene she'd thought she left behind in LA.

Body rigid with tension, she walked across the main living area of the rustic and yet somehow chic A-frame and leaned against the front door, pulling her attention away from the victim and to the room as a whole. Since the front door was slightly ajar when the victim was found, chances are the perp entered the home right here. A wisp of hair slipped loose from her ponytail. Laney smoothed it back, her gloved hand shaking, giving away the dread and uncertainty building inside her.

How the hell did this happen?

Shutter Lake, the perfect little village—according to countless lifestyle magazines—nestled amid the Sierra Mountains of northern California, now had its first murder. Anticipation roiling with uncertainty had her wrapping her arms around her waist to hold her body still. Worse, this was no poor wandering homeless person or visitor or newcomer to the area splayed on the floor. This was a lifetime resident, beloved by everyone—a daughter, business owner, and model perfect citizen.

Sylvia Cole, twenty-six years old and stunningly beautiful, was dead. *Murdered*. No question about that. Laney had seen more than her share of homicide victims in her former life. The life she'd left behind in search of peace, quiet and a slower pace.

Another burst of frustration laced with dread heaved from her lungs. As deputy chief of police, she was the closest thing to a detective assigned to Shutter Lake's tiny department. There was the chief, Griff McCabe, who'd grown up in Shutter Lake. He'd joined the force following a two-year criminal justice program with an emphasis on the collection of evidence. His father, the former chief of police, often laughed and boasted that when other kids were learning to play t-ball, his one and only son was honing his skills in surveillance and keeping the peace. The old man had one thing right, about the only pastime available to cops around this town was keeping an eye on residents and their homes and businesses.

The occasional burglary occurred—always a perpetrator from outside of town. Someone passing through or a homeless person from a new camp in the woods beyond the city limits. Now and again a fender bender occurred, but that was generally handled between the drivers. Once in a great while a citizen had too much to drink and decided to stagger home rather than to call a taxi and ended up trying to enter the wrong house or ended up sleeping it off on a park bench. Even those instances were few and far between.

In reality, beyond the initial required training, Shutter Lake's police force was nothing more than glorified mall rent-a-cops. Keeping an eye on things and occasionally nudging a citizen who misbehaved to watch his or her step. Laney had driven folks home from local pubs, she'd watched after their houses while they were traveling—even fed their birds and fish from time to time. The truth was, Shutter Lake hadn't needed a seasoned detective like her. A seen-it-all former LAPD detective, at that. But she'd come here—to this paradise tucked in the valley—twenty-four months and one week ago badly needing the calm and tranquility the town offered. McCabe had been glad to have her on board. So much so he'd given her an impressive title to go with an unexpectedly generous salary.

Now it seemed they were going to need the special skill set she had hoped never again to drag out of retirement.

"Focus, Laney." With both hands she grabbed the gritty cop instincts she'd once trusted completely and hauled them from the black hole where she'd tossed them two years ago. She'd promised herself she was never going back there. Never.

The home's front door had been unlocked and ajar when one of the victim's employees, one Renata Fernandez, arrived at the house to see what was keeping the boss this chilly Thursday morning. No indication of forced entry at that door or any other potential access points into the home.

Sylvia Cole, owner and operator of a local house cleaning service called Sparkle, was usually in her downtown office by six every morning, Monday through Saturday. When she hadn't shown by seven-thirty, Fernandez had come looking for her. Fernandez had given her statement and was currently sequestered to the back deck. She'd told Officer Trask she couldn't be in the house with her friend lying dead on the floor.

Laney glanced beyond the wall of windows on the other side of the room. The woman sat in one of the four metal chairs flanking a table on the expansive deck. Her cell phone was in Laney's pocket. She didn't want Fernandez calling anyone and discussing what she'd found.

Fortunately, once the lady had called the police, she'd been too distraught to think to call the Cole family or anyone else from Sparkle. Trask had arrived on the scene to find her kneeling on the floor next to the victim, deep in prayer as she rocked back and forth.

Sylvia Cole's arms were spread out to her sides, her legs slightly bent at the knees and angled to her right, her left hip prominent. Laney's first impression was that the body had been posed. The victim's long blond hair fanned around her head, her blue eyes stared unseeing at the steeply vaulted ceiling where a fan slowly turned. Her pink nightshirt sporting the Sparkle logo was hiked up to the tops of her thighs. When Laney crouched down for a closer look she noted the victim wore lavender panties. No bruising on the thighs or other visible indication of sexual assault.

No blood. No visible physical injury at all beyond the ring of bruises circling her neck. Laney didn't need a coroner or a forensics expert to tell her the woman had been strangled. There were no ligature marks suggesting a rope or a scarf or belt. The bruises were unquestionably made by the killer's hands. Laney had seen it before. Pinpoint hemorrhages in the whites of the eyes suggested the same, manual strangulation.

This murder was close up, perhaps executed by an intimate of the victim since there was no sign of forced entry. Despite Shutter Lake's peaceful reputation, folks weren't naïve. Some of the most brilliant minds in the world lived in this small town. They locked their doors. And, maybe the oddest part of all, no indication the victim fought her attacker. As far as Laney could see there was no skin under her meticulously manicured nails. No bruises or other marks on her arms.

"Shit," Laney muttered again.

She shook her head. If the killer was someone the victim knew, then in all probability he—and it was most likely a he—lived right here in Shutter Lake.

Clearing her mind of the disturbing thought, Laney absorbed the details of the room. The chair that had stood at an angle to the sofa was overturned. A teakwood tray, clay potted African violet and a magazine had been swiped or knocked off the ottoman that served as a coffee table. Potting soil from the shattered container had spilled across the floor. The victim's purse lay on the floor by the table closest to the door. A wooden bowl atop that table held wads of keys. In addition to the usual car and house keys, the victim had keys to her office, to her clients' homes and businesses. Laney hoped her clients' keys were locked up in the office downtown. Sparkle serviced the who's who of Shutter Lake.

Her wallet was empty of cash and credit cards. A hairbrush, lip gloss, a tampon that looked as if it had been in her purse for ages, and a bottle of over the counter pain medication had been unceremoniously dumped on the floor along with half a dozen of her business cards.

One of the cards, the side that featured Sylvia Cole's gorgeous smile turned up, lay next to the pile. So young. Damn.

The rest of the main living area was undisturbed. Laptop sat on the dining table, opened to the online boutique where she'd been viewing holiday wear. No dishes in the sink, no clutter on the counters. No stacks of this and that on the dining table. Even the fridge was pristine. Wine, cheese, fruit and a box filled with tempting cupcakes from the local bakery were neatly organized. Evidently the queen of clean kept her own abode sparkling, too.

The small house had two bedrooms and two baths beyond the expansive main living area. Bedroom one and the smaller bathroom were located to the left of the dining area while the master suite was to the right of the living room. With another glance at the woman on the deck, Laney headed down a short hall to the master bedroom. This bedroom also looked out onto the back deck that spanned the length of the house. French doors were locked. Two towering windows looked out onto the woods that butted both ends as well as the back of the property.

On the bed pale blue sheets were tousled as if the victim had already been tucked in for the night when her killer arrived. Or maybe she'd been in bed with her killer. Using both gloved hands, Laney picked up the twisted flat sheet and sniffed it. Perfume—she glanced at the bottle of Angel on the dresser, the vic's—and something more masculine. A combination of leather and something citrusy, maybe lemon. Definitely men's cologne. The faint white stains on the fitted sheet would tell the tale of what took place in the bed most recently. Not that Laney had any doubts about her own conclusions.

On the bedside table a cell phone was plugged in to charge. Laney picked it up and scanned the calls and texts. Nothing since six yesterday evening until about six-thirty this morning. Sylvia either didn't communicate with anyone during that time or those particular contacts had been deleted by the killer.

Beyond the tousled sheets, the bedroom appeared to be in order. No strewn clothes or overturned furniture. She ventured into the en suite bath. The pristine tile walls of the shower were dry, a loofah lay on the marble bench and a towel hung over the glass door. The terry cloth was dry to the touch.

A walk through the closet showed a chic wardrobe impeccably organized. The jewelry box on the built-in bureau was overturned. Costume jewelry pieces lay scattered on the smooth white surface. Any fine jewelry was gone. Laney would need a family member or friend to determine what, if anything, was missing.

She wandered back to the main living area. The victim had money, no doubt. She'd started her business right out of high school with nothing but a broom and a bottle of window cleaner, she'd touted in her locally run commercials. By the time she was twenty-one she had an office downtown and a six-woman crew. Her only competitor had packed up and left town that same year and no other cleaning service had dared invade Sparkle's territory.

But if a burglar was after money—Laney paused to consider the victim once more—why not choose the home of someone else in Shutter Lake? There were dozens of far wealthier residents.

Access.

Laney's gaze strayed to the security system's keypad. Generic, definitely not high end. According to the monitoring company, the system had not been activated in the past twenty-four hours. Why have a security system if you weren't going to use it? Yet, lots of people had one installed and rarely used it. They loved the idea of having one, felt some sense of security just knowing it was available. But it didn't work if it wasn't activated.

Either way, Sylvia Cole likely knew the person who killed her. Clearly she opened the door to him or her. Laney was leaning toward a male perpetrator considering the semen stains on the sheets.

If the motive was nothing more than robbery, why not take any number of other highly marketable items—like the laptop on the dining table, or the latest video game console on a shelf right under the television in the living room? This didn't have the feel of a robbery.

This was a murder staged to look as if a robbery attempt had gone very wrong.

As if she'd said the words out loud, the woman on the deck stood and turned toward the wall of windows. Her gaze landed first on the victim lying on the floor. Fernandez's body visibly shook. Finally her attention shifted to Laney. She was afraid. Afraid of what the future held for her now that the owner of the business that represented her livelihood was dead, and devastated by the abrupt and unexpected loss of her longtime friend.

Laney walked toward the French doors that separated the stylish interior from the rustic outdoors. This home was an accurate depiction of the woman who had lived here. The interior reflected her taste in the finer things. But then, why not? Sylvia Cole was the only child of wealthy parents. A young woman born with the proverbial silver spoon in her mouth. Yet, as an adult, she had chosen to work hard and make her own way, even forgoing the Ivy League education both her parents had attained and offered to provide for her.

Sylvia Cole had been her own person and completely confident in who she was.

The air was crisp on the deck. The woman, Renata Fernandez, was the victim's second in command at Sparkle. Fernandez had been with the service since the beginning. Like the victim, she was young, maybe twenty-five or six, and beautiful. One couldn't help noticing that all those employed by Sparkle were young and beautiful. Was that a prerequisite of employment? If so, why? Were these ladies providing more than cleaning service?

Slow down, Laney, you're allowing your own dark experience to color your conclusions.

"Ms. Fernandez, it's a little brisk out here. Are you sure

you wouldn't rather be inside? We could go to the guest room."

Fernandez shook her head. "No. Please. I can't go back in there."

Laney nodded. "I understand." She pulled out her cell and sent Trask a text to bring coffee when he returned. Fernandez needed warning up and Laney could use a second cup herself. "Would you like to sit, Ms. Fernandez, or do you prefer to stand?"

This time of year the temps dropped into the forties, occasionally lower, at night. Laney would just as soon stand as to sit in one of the metal chairs but she would defer to the other woman's wishes.

"Thank you, Deputy Holt. I prefer to stand." As she said the words she turned just enough that the interior of the house was no longer in her line of sight.

"Ms. Fernandez, how long did you know Sylvia?" Laney knew the answers to many of the questions she intended to ask, but she needed the witness's confirmation. The more mundane questions also helped to put the other person at ease.

Fernandez hugged her arms around herself much as Laney had done earlier. "Please call me Renata." She drew in a deep, shuddering breath. "We met at a club in Grass Valley when we were in high school." She shook her head. "We both had fake IDs so we could get beer." Her cheeks flushed. "You know how it is when you're that young. You're foolish and eager for the rest of your life to happen as quickly as possible."

Laney nodded. "I did the same thing. I hated all the guys my own age. Older guys were far more interesting. They didn't hang around the skating rink or the bowling alley."

Fernandez nodded, her smile sad. "That's why we went to the clubs."

She fell silent for a moment. Swiped at her eyes with the wad of tissues in her hand.

A faint smile tilted her lips and she went on. "We became friends and she told me about her plans to start her own business. She had no desire to go to college the way her parents wanted. She talked her mother into giving her the college money to start her business and for a down payment on her home." Fernandez looked around. "She bought this place when she was nineteen years old. She ran the business from right here for two years. Then we moved into the office downtown."

"Were the two of you partners?" Again, Laney had the answer but she wanted to know more about their relationship. The best way to get all the right information was to ask all the wrong questions. Most people would go to great lengths to correct your mistakes, always adding more than requested in the process.

"No. I'm just like the rest of the crew, an employee, but we were best friends."

"Did you feel as if after all this time you should have been more?"

Surprise flared in her eyes. "Of course not! The business was her idea. Her idea and her execution. I was just along for the ride. I feel honored that she asked me to be her right hand. I was very grateful she had so much faith in me when she made the offer. She pays me way more than I'm worth and treats—treated me," her voice warbled, "with respect and admiration."

Laney reached into her jacket pocket and retrieved her notepad, flipped to a fresh page then dug in that same pocket for her pen. "What about the other employees? Can you give me their names, cell numbers and addresses?"

Fernandez swiped at her nose and cleared her throat. "Of course." She frowned for a moment. "I actually have all their contact information in my phone. Would you like me to share those five contacts with you? Their addresses are in the notes section. All of them are at work this morning."

"That would be great." Technology was an amazing thing. "Do you recall an employee, past or present, having trouble with Sylvia? Pay disputes or assignment issues?"

Fernandez's chin lifted in defiance of any suggestion of discord. "Never. She paid us all well. Used our personalities and strong points to choose assignments." Her expression hardened in challenge. "Maybe you don't know this, but Sylvia made it a point to hire people who might not have a chance at a good life otherwise. She sought out those less fortunate. She was an angel."

Laney had a reasonably clear idea what she meant, but she wanted her conclusions confirmed. "How do you mean less fortunate?"

"We were all undocumented when we were hired. Most of us didn't have a real home or food on a regular basis. Sylvia helped us with the paperwork for citizenship. She helped us find better places to live. I'm the only one who lives in Shutter Lake. The others commute in together from the Grass Valley area, but they have nice places. Two even own their own homes."

"So all of you owe Sylvia a great deal?" Fernandez nodded in answer to Laney's question. "Do you have any idea who might want to harm her? Did she ever have trouble with anyone outside the business? Maybe she mentioned someone who was bothering her."

Obviously someone had. Of course there was always the chance the murder had been an act of impulse or of opportunity if the robber hadn't known Sylvia was at home when he chose her place to burgle.

Except that Laney had a feeling this was not about a few pieces of jewelry or a handful of cash and plastic.

Her investigative skills might be a little rusty but not that out of shape.

Fernandez shook her head adamantly. "Everyone loved Sylvie. I never knew her to have a harsh exchange with anyone."

Laney thought of the rumpled sheets. "What about a boyfriend? Was Sylvia seeing anyone?"

"I don't think so." The other woman considered the question for a minute. "Sylvie—that's what her friends called her—was very independent. She didn't want anyone telling her what to do, not even her parents. She made up her own mind and did what she pleased. She didn't want to be tied down with a husband or children." She smiled, the expression not quite so sad this time. "I told her one of these days that clock of hers would start ticking and she would marry the first man who looked her way."

"Sylvia was young and beautiful and," Laney began, highlighting all that the witness had said about the victim, "as you said very independent, but she would still have needs."

Another flush crept up Fernandez's cheeks. "This is true, yes. But if there was anyone special she never talked about it with me. She was very private about that aspect of her personal life. She liked keeping her home life and work life separate."

So much for her friend having a clue about the victim's lover. With any luck, DNA would give them a place to start. But that was only if the semen on those sheets led back to someone in one of the databases at their disposal. Prints would be useful as well. The problem was, all those things took time. Even in a small town like Shutter Lake, determining who might have been involved with the victim would take time—particularly if that someone didn't want to be discovered.

Chief of Police Griff McCabe was also their forensic tech. He'd been the official evidence collector in Shutter Lake for nearly two decades. Most of the time that duty encompassed nothing more than gathering prints and sending them to the lab in Sacramento. But this was different.

Way different.

Inside, the front door opened and the chief walked in, Trask, carrying a drink tray with four coffees, followed right on his heels. Laney flashed a smile for Fernandez. "Officer Trask brought you a coffee to warm you up. I'll send him out."

Fernandez thanked her and Laney gave her a reassuring smile. Hopefully she would eventually recall any disagreements the victim had with coworkers or any potential romantic interests. No one went through life without roadblocks or obstacles and certainly not without heartbreak.

No one was that perfect. Not even the people who lived in Shutter Lake.

Laney and McCabe met near the victim. One look at his unshaven face and blood shot eyes and she knew her original deduction was correct, he'd had a bad night. Not that he ever looked much different at nine in the morning. It was usually noon before he resembled anything fit for human interaction. Not that she was judging. For months after she left L.A. she had been a mess. Her drug of choice had been endorphins. She'd run morning, noon and night, pushing her body beyond its limits.

She still ran five miles or so every night. Kept her sane. Kept the memories out of her dreams.

McCabe shook his head, exhaled a big breath. "What do we have?"

"Missing credit cards and any cash that was in her wallet. Jewelry box has been searched. Few things knocked around and this." Laney stared down at the victim. "Looks like she was strangled. Maybe she interrupted the burglary in progress. Doesn't make a whole lot of sense since the perp dumped her purse. The fact that it was here should have signaled that the owner was as well. I'm surprised he didn't cut and run. Her cell phone is on the bedside table. No calls or texts since around six last evening until her friend," Laney gestured to the woman outside, "started calling her this morning."

McCabe set his hands on his hips. "I called the coroner. He'll be here within the hour." He shook his head. "I've known this girl my whole life. I'm calling in the county crime scene unit. This is out of my league."

Laney agreed. "So far nothing from any of the neighbors." Another of their officers was canvassing the people who lived on this street but neighbors were few and far between. The chances that anyone saw or heard one damned thing were about nil. "The robbery scenario doesn't feel right. Too many easy to move items left behind. After he killed her, why not grab the laptop and the game console?"

McCabe forked his fingers through his hair. "Doesn't make sense. This," he gestured to the dead girl on the floor, "doesn't make sense. I gotta talk to her parents."

Laney didn't envy him that task. "You want me to stay on things here?"

His bleary gaze met hers. "The truth? I'd rather you come with me."

Great. "I should take Renata Fernandez home on the way. She's been here for hours. She's already given her statement. I don't think there's anything else she can tell us right now. Maybe when she's had a chance to get past the shock, she'll recall more."

"I don't want her talking to anyone," McCabe said. "Not until we know how the hell this happened. Make sure she understands."

"I'll make sure." Laney took one last look around. Things like this didn't happen in Shutter Lake.

Until now.

CHAPTER TWO

Zion and Yolanda Cole's home was on the opposite side of town from their daughter's. The property was considered a mini ranch; it spanned nearly a hundred acres, much of which extended into the mountains. Horses and goats grazed in the pasture. A classic horse barn sat in the distance.

The animals paid little attention as Laney and McCabe followed the stone walkway to the house. In the front yard chickens eyed them speculatively, their clucking seemingly sending up a warning that something bad was coming. This was the house where Sylvia Cole grew up as an only child. Laney's gaze settled on the double front doors as she and McCabe took the final steps up to the broad stone porch. This day—this moment—would forever change the older couple's lives. Nothing in their world would ever be the same.

This was the worst part of being a cop.

McCabe rang the bell.

The two of them had rendezvoused at City Hall so as not to descend upon the Cole home in two vehicles. While she'd taken Fernandez home, McCabe had shaved and popped drops into his eyes. One of the first things Laney had noticed about her new boss two years ago was that he kept a change of clothes, including an extra shirt, along with an electric razor, eye drops and mouthwash in his locker. Walking through the small locker room was necessary to reach the bathrooms at City Hall. No one bothered to secure their lockers and half the time the doors popped open if they weren't closed just right. Most of the lockers were stocked pretty much like Laney's—a heavy jacket, snow boots and not much else.

After a few months in Shutter Lake, Laney realized that McCabe slept in the office occasionally—usually when he'd gone to one of the pubs and gotten hammered. Walking to City Hall was far safer than driving or staggering home.

Today she was particularly grateful for McCabe's stash of personal items. The parents of the victim didn't need to hear about her murder from a man who looked hungover.

Yolanda answered the door. Surprise flashed in her expression, immediately followed by uncertainty. "Chief McCabe." Despite her obvious misgivings, she smiled at Laney. "Deputy Holt. What brings you here this morning?"

Yolanda Cole was closer to sixty than fifty but, like her daughter, she was trim and attractive. Her gray cashmere sweater and matching wide leg trousers were a near perfect match to her hair and she looked nothing short of elegant.

"Ma'am," McCabe said, "is Mr. Cole at home?"

Her surprise and uncertainty gave way to something more relaxed. "He is. Please, come in." She opened the door wide and waited for them to enter. "He's on the deck having coffee." She closed the door and looked from one to the other. "Would either of you like coffee?"

"No, thank you, ma'am."

Laney shook her head. "I'm good, thanks." That second cup she'd guzzled already had her guts in a knot.

"Very well. This way." As Mrs. Cole strode across the great room that encompassed the living, dining and kitchen space, she said, "I'm sure Zion and the rest of the council are still fussing over those plans for the remodel of City Hall." She paused at the French doors that made up a part of the wall of windows facing the lush landscape beyond the house. "The two of you should remind him that they've had long enough to consider all the contractor bids."

Talk of updating City Hall had started around the time Laney arrived. Money wasn't an issue. Shutter Lake had the funds and several residents, including the Coles, had thrown in very generous six figure donations. But like every other aspect of bureaucracy these matters were slow moving.

McCabe managed a dim smile. "I'll be sure to do that, but just now we need to speak to you as well, Mrs. Cole."

The uncertainty slipped back onto her face. "Oh, of course."

She opened the door. "Zion, we have company. Chief McCabe and Deputy Holt are here."

Zion Cole stood. He reached for Laney's hand first, gave it a quick shake, then moved on to McCabe's. He held on a little longer to the chief's, gave it a couple of strong pumps. "I told the council you two were going to start making house calls if we didn't get the ball rolling on those renovation plans."

"I'm sure everyone will be happy to see us bringing City Hall into the current century," McCabe said.

"Have a seat." Cole gestured to the many decadently upholstered chairs neatly arranged about the deck to take advantage of the massive stone fireplace as well as the beautiful view.

Laney sat closest to Mrs. Cole. McCabe took a seat across the coffee table from her husband.

"I need to ask you a few questions about Sylvia."

McCabe said these words gently. He generally spoke quietly. Laney considered him a man of few words most often expressed in soft tones. He had that Clint Eastwood charisma. Raising his voice wasn't necessary but you recognized in a heartbeat when he was not happy. So far she was yet to see any of his officers defy his orders. Even when she occasionally questioned his tactics, he spoke calmly and reasonably when he responded to her queries. Frankly, she hadn't once witnessed him losing his temper. His uncompromising ability to keep his cool was so not in keeping with his inability to control his drinking. Then again, the only downside she'd noticed with the issue was his coming in a little late some days. But he was there so it wasn't like his tardiness was a problem.

Bottom line, he was a good man who cared about his community.

Even now, with this murder looming over their heads, he looked and sounded relaxed. The white shirt he'd slipped on at the office was fresh, crisp. The leather jacket he wore was well worn like his jeans and boots, giving him a laid back appearance. Despite the easygoing facade, he still had a commanding air about him. The wealthiest of residents in Shutter Lake respected him.

Griff McCabe was a true paradox. So controlled on the job and yet so out of control after hours.

Laney had no right to judge. She presented the disguise of being the tough female cop with the big city experience who lived her life exactly the way she wanted.

Not entirely accurate.

There was nothing like a murder to send a person down the road of self-analysis.

"Is my daughter in some sort of trouble?" Cole asked.

His wife's hands went to her face. "Please tell us she's all right."

"Has Sylvia mentioned any trouble recently with a client or an employee?" McCabe ventured, carefully side-stepping their questions.

Mrs. Cole reached for her husband's hand, her eyes wide with worry.

There was no way to save them from this devastating moment.

"Not that I'm aware." Cole looked to his wife. She shook her head. He turned back to McCabe. "What's this about?"

"What about a boyfriend?" Laney asked. The longer she and McCabe could avoid giving the bad news the more likely the Coles were to provide accurate answers. Once the truth was out, devastation would take over and extracting reliable answers would be next to impossible. It was a terribly clinical way to view the situation but finding Sylvia Cole's murderer had to be priority one.

Mrs. Cole shook her head again. "Sylvia doesn't have a boyfriend. She hasn't had one since high school. She's very independent. She likes having sole dominion over her life." The older woman laughed softly, the sound almost painful. "I've reconciled myself to the idea that I may never have grandchildren."

Cole patted his wife's hand. "Our daughter is still plenty young enough for that to happen in the future, dear."

The swell of regret tightened Laney's throat.

"You're not aware of anyone who pays particular

attention to Sylvia?" McCabe posed this question to the victim's father.

"No. Not in a negative or unkind way. You know as well as I do that everyone loves Sylvia." He shrugged his broad shoulders. "What is this about, Griff?"

"She hasn't come to you recently for money? No issues with her business?"

"No." Zion Cole stared directly at McCabe now. "Tell me what the hell is going on."

"Mr. Cole." Laney didn't know what possessed her to take it from there. Maybe the cloud of grief that had suddenly shadowed McCabe's face or maybe just his hesitation. "Mrs. Cole." Laney shifted her attention between the two. "We've just come from Sylvia's home. I am so sorry to tell you this, but she's dead."

Zion Cole shot to his feet, horror and shock aimed at McCabe. "Is this true?"

Mrs. Cole stared at Laney for what felt like an eternity before she burst into tears.

While Laney rushed back to the living room for the box of tissues she'd seen on an end table, she heard McCabe say, "I'm sorry, sir, but yes, it's true. The coroner should be with her by now and hopefully we'll soon know more about what happened."

"I'm going over there."

Zion Cole executed an about face and strode toward the French doors. Laney blocked his path, the impotent box of tissues in her hand. "Mr. Cole, you can't go to your daughter's home right now."

McCabe steadied Mrs. Cole as she swayed on her feet. "We need to see her." The words were an agonizing wail.

"Please," Laney urged the man towering over her, "there are things we need to explain first."

Zion Cole gave Laney his back and returned to the

chair he had abandoned, though he didn't sit. McCabe ushered Mrs. Cole back into her chair.

When McCabe hesitated the older man finally took his seat. "We can't confirm anything until we have the coroner's preliminary findings," McCabe explained. "But you need to be aware that we're treating Sylvia's death as a homicide."

Mrs. Cole gasped. "Someone murdered her?"

"We believe so," Laney said. It was best not to go too deep into that area just now. "Her front door was standing open and some of her things were disturbed. Like her purse and her jewelry box. Can you tell us, Mrs. Cole, if Sylvia had any fine jewelry? Anything particularly valuable in the house that we should be looking for?"

Mrs. Cole shook her head, her lips trembling. "Nothing I can think of just now." Tears streamed down her face.

"Someone robbed and murdered my daughter?"

Mr. Cole's words echoed in the morning air, the sound loaded with anguish.

"That's the way it looks right now," McCabe said. "Our officers are talking to the neighbors and we'll be interviewing all her employees. We're hoping someone will know something that can help us find the person who did this. So far everyone agrees that Sylvia didn't have any enemies, no boyfriend. No trouble personally or professionally. That leaves us with a random intruder."

Mr. Cole's expression hardened to granite. "So what you're telling us is that you don't have any evidence. You don't have any idea who did this?"

A trauma-filled beat passed with nothing but the sound of Mrs. Cole's sobs expanding between them.

"No, sir," McCabe admitted. "We don't have anything at this time. We hope to find prints or some other evidence that will help in our search, but we've got nothing right now."

Before the older man could launch the anger now seizing his face, Laney said, "But we've only just begun, sir. It's rare to have any leads at this stage."

Zion Cole stared at Laney. Like every other member of the Shutter Lake City Council, he was aware of her background. She had a stellar resume from the Los Angeles Police Department. She'd spent her final two years in L.A. working homicide. This tragic event was nothing new to her. She hoped that knowledge proved some comfort to the grieving man.

"Just promise me you'll find who did this. That's all I want to hear."

"We'll do everything in our power," Laney assured him. "Chief McCabe has already taken every necessary step to ensure we have all the backup we need. The county's crime scene unit is en route as we speak."

"We've got this under control, Zion," McCabe assured him. "Trust me on that. We will find him."

"I need to see her," Mrs. Cole said. "I need to see her before they start cutting on her."

"I'll talk to the coroner's office and make the arrangements." McCabe reached for her hand, gave it a squeeze. "I'll see that no one touches Sylvia before you have some time with her."

Laney went over the procedures that would follow with Mrs. Cole while Mr. Cole questioned McCabe further about how the investigation would be conducted. Sylvia's parents were both putting on a fairly brave face but Laney understood the collapse would come after she and McCabe were out of the way.

Ten minutes later the anguished sobs of the parents followed Laney and McCabe as they exited the Cole home. Laney exiled the sounds as they made their way along the stone walkway. Her focus on this investigation could not be splintered by emotion. Every damned member of the department was a lifetime resident of this town—except her. She couldn't get caught up in the emotional side of this tragedy.

They climbed into McCabe's decades old, fully restored Ford Bronco. The man liked his classic vehicles. He had a Mustang from the sixties and a Ford truck from the fifties, all in immaculate condition. When they were first getting to know each other, he'd told Laney that everyone should have a hobby. Maybe that was her problem. She had never taken the time for hobbies. The closest things she had to hobbies was her fixation with the firing range and her determination to outdo her own record when it came to endurance runs.

But she learned a couple of years ago that those things didn't count.

"Thanks for jumping in when I hesitated."

She glanced at the man behind the wheel. "You've known these people your whole life. This can't be easy." Not to mention this was his first homicide. The first one was always the hardest.

"That's why I need you to be lead on this, Holt." He sent her a sideways glance. "You have experience. I got nothing."

"You have instincts about the people you know," she countered. "You have no idea how much difference that makes."

The words weren't just to make him feel better. The more an investigator knew about a victim and those around that victim, the better the chance of finding the truth. There were times, like this one, where that knowledge presented a double-edged sword. McCabe's connection to the victim and her family also came with emotional baggage and certain expectations.

Any and all expectations had to be thrown out the window. People were rarely exactly who you thought they were. A good cop had to look beyond the expected to the carefully shielded part beneath the surface.

"Maybe," McCabe said. "But I still want you to be lead. You can stay emotionally detached. I'm not sure I can."

Laney thought about the one time she'd had a somewhat personal encounter with the victim. Maybe three, three and a half months ago, sometime in July. She'd gone to Johnny's for beer and pizza. It was a weekday night so the place wasn't that crowded. Sylvia had been there with a friend. Laney later learned that the Hispanic girl was her newest employee. Sylvia was well beyond buzzed that night. She was seriously drunk. The younger woman whose name Laney couldn't remember had been trying to get her to quiet down, but Sylvia was having no part of it. One of the two had apparently just broken up with some guy or something. Whatever the case Sylvia was on a roll about what jerks men could be.

The second time Laney saw the manager go over to the table and ask Sylvia to settle down, she felt compelled to intercede—even though she was off duty. She joined the ladies at their table. Sylvia at first ignored her but then she'd ranted on about how she hated men. Laney had suggested that she take the two home. It was late, after all. Sylvia argued for a minute, maybe two, but she'd come around. On the drive to her house she had grown quiet and withdrawn. The other girl's English wasn't so good and she hardly talked at all. Laney suspected she was afraid of being asked for some sort of ID.

Once they had reached Sylvia's house she had grown belligerent again. She'd ranted at Laney about how the Shutter Lake police were worthless. They wouldn't know a bad guy if one stumbled into City Hall. Laney hadn't argued with her. It was best not to try and reason with a drunk. It was a battle rarely won by anyone. Instead, she helped the friend get Sylvia inside and urged her to make sure she stayed inside until she sobered up. The younger woman nodded her understanding and Laney went home.

She hadn't thought about that night since. Now Laney wondered if she should have asked Sylvia what she meant by bad guy. Had she gotten involved with someone who was into some illegal activity? Was that the kind of *bad* she meant? Or was she just pissed at her guy and considered him a different kind of bad? Laney had a feeling Sylvia was far too smart to get mixed up with a jerk of a guy even when she was inebriated.

By the time they reached Olive Tree Lane both hers and McCabe's cell phones were buzzing.

"Holt." Laney answered hers, turning toward the window so as not to talk over McCabe who'd answered his.

"Ma'am, this is Trask. I think I found something you need to see."

Evidently McCabe received the same news. The Bronco went from rolling along at the posted speed limit to barreling down the tree lined two-lane road as if he'd just entered the Indy 500.

The coroner's van was already on site and so was the crime scene unit. McCabe pulled over to the side of the road next to the Shutter Lake police cruiser since the driveway was packed with the other official vehicles.

Laney followed McCabe up the walk and into the house. Sylvia's body was already bagged and on a gurney.

"Hey, Tom," McCabe said, "you got anything on time of death?"

Tom Parker, one of the Nevada County coroners, was in his mid to late fifties, blond hair with plenty of gray sprinkled in and the tanned, lean physique of someone who spent a lot of time in outdoor activities.

He nodded to Laney before answering. "I'd say she's been dead around twelve to fifteen hours, maybe a little more, between nine last night and midnight would be a safe estimate."

"Manual strangulation?" Laney asked.

"Looks that way but you know I can't say for sure until we complete the autopsy."

"Any question in your mind whether or not this was a homicide?" McCabe asked.

Parker shook his head. "None at all. But we'll run the usual tests, check her blood alcohol level, look for drugs and sexual activity, anything else out of the ordinary. I'll give you everything I can as quickly as possible. I can well imagine how difficult this is going to be for your community."

No one ever got used to murder, but in cities like L.A it was never a surprise to hear about it on the news.

Shutter Lake was nothing like LA. This was going to rock the community.

"Thanks, Tom. The parents want to see her before you start the autopsy. Can you take care of that?"

"Sure will," Tom assured him.

McCabe shifted his attention to Trask who waited at the entrance of the small hallway that lead to the master suite.

Laney watched the coroner and his assistant leave with

the body before following McCabe and Trask. She heaved a big breath and glanced over at the guys in the white suits who were dusting for prints and searching for other trace elements of potential evidence. Their rhythmic movements prompted far too many bad memories for her comfort.

By the time she caught up with McCabe, he and Trask were in the victim's sizeable walk-in closet.

"As I made a final walk-thru of the house before the crime scene investigators got started," he was explaining, "I thought it might be a good idea to look behind all these clothes." He indicted the line of blouses and tees hanging in a colorful row. "You know, just to make sure we weren't overlooking anything that might be relevant."

McCabe nodded and motioned for the younger man to get on with it.

"When I got to this row," he reached up and parted the garments, "I found this."

Behind the silk and cashmere tops was a wall safe. Not so surprising. Laney imagined most of the houses in Shutter Lake had hidden safes. Admittedly this one was considerably larger than average. She moved closer as Trask reached for the door.

"It wasn't even closed all the way." He glanced back as he opened it. "I think maybe this might be important."

Once the safe stood open, the officer stepped aside so that McCabe and Laney could move in closer. The steel box in the wall was a little deeper than Laney had expected. A full foot at least and noticeably larger all the way around than the average ones she'd seen.

"What's behind this wall?" she asked, still reeling with surprise at the contents staring her in the face.

"There's a coat closet on the other side of this wall. I checked," Trask said. "Behind the coats you can see the outline of this thing. You know, anyone could have reached right in and taken all that."

He was right. Evidently the person who killed Sylvia Cole had no idea the safe existed.

"I don't believe I've ever seen one this big," McCabe said, almost to himself.

But it wasn't really the size of the safe that was so stunning.

It was the stacks and stacks of bundled cash sitting inside it.

CHAPTER THREE

Chief of Police McCabe surveyed the crowd gathered in front of City Hall for a long moment before he spoke. This was another task Laney didn't envy him. Rumor of some terrible event, of course, had spread like a wildfire. The phones hadn't stopped ringing.

People were worried and afraid.

"At eight o'clock this morning Shutter Lake resident Sylvia Cole was found murdered in her home." He said the words clearly and with surprising strength. The disbelief had worn off and the anger had set in.

A rumble went through the crowd. The rumor had swept along the town's grapevine, feeding the frenzy. Whatever story they heard, people instinctively understood that something very bad had happened, but no one knew exactly what.

Until now.

Laney stood next to the parents while McCabe relayed the carefully worded press release. Three reporters from Sacramento had shown up for the press conference. Another one was from Grass Valley as well as an additional five—no six—from various other nearby towns. Between this morning's summons of the crime scene unit and a coroner and the noontime announcement that there would be a press conference at five, word had gotten around.

The story would no doubt run on the national news when folks connected the event with the many articles about the best small towns in the country that had run just two months ago in several major magazines. The urge to pack up and go off into the mountains for a long, soul-cleansing retreat was a palpable force inside Laney.

Stiffening her spine against the old panic that wanted to gnaw at her, Laney focused on the crowd. Killers often liked to put in an appearance at press conferences related to their work. Sometimes they even showed up outside a crime scene, hanging around in the gathered crowd feigning shocked curiosity.

She scanned each face, noted the names of those she recognized. So far all were residents save the half dozen or so reporters. No one, least of all Laney, wanted to believe anyone who lived in Shutter Lake was capable of murder. But she wasn't a fool and rose-colored glasses had never been one of her preferred accessories.

If pushed just the right way for just long enough, almost everyone was capable of violence.

Laney spotted Julia Ford and wondered if she was here as a resident or if she was representing the Firefly, Shutter Lake's weekly newspaper. Carrie Stone, the owner of the small paper, was traveling in Europe. The Firefly focused on community news and events with a small classifieds section and the occasional obituary. Julia Ford's lifestyle column that ran in the Sacramento Bee was also featured in the Firefly. Like Laney, Julia had her own dark history with murder.

Julia stared straight at Laney as if she'd sensed she was

thinking about her. Laney gave her a nod and moved on to the next face in the sizeable crowd. There would be questions at their next girls' night out.

Next to Laney, Yolanda Cole quaked with the effort of holding back the breakdown she'd had only minutes before the press conference began. The poor woman had cried until her face was a red, swollen mask. Though Laney most likely would never have children of her own, she had two nieces. She couldn't imagine the horror of losing one of them. Even a hard-assed cop like her had a heart.

On the other side of Mrs. Cole was her husband. He stood tall, shoulders back, face a veneer of somberness. His breakdown had happened at his home this morning as Laney and McCabe left. He wanted to be strong for his wife, for his lost daughter. Any father would want to do so. It wasn't difficult to zero in on his agenda: find the son of a bitch who did this and make him pay. She imagined if their investigation failed to bring this nightmare to a speedy conclusion that Cole would hire a private investigator. She couldn't blame him. He possessed the means, why not? A reputable PI could be an asset to an investigation. God knew a resourceful PI could cross lines a good cop wouldn't think of crossing.

Laney flinched. Just another little something from her past that she had no desire to revisit. She hadn't always been a good cop when it came to not crossing lines. Sometimes to get the job done you had to step over a line here or there.

Murder was a very good reason for ignoring the rules.

Not going to happen this time, Laney.

She recalled the promises she'd made to herself when she put L.A. in her rearview mirror. No more pushing the boundaries. No more allowing the job to take over her life.

No more pretending it didn't matter if she survived as long as she got the bad guy.

Balance. The word echoed through her. Months of therapy had driven that word home. Funny how she just couldn't seem to keep her mental footing no matter how hard she tried. One of these days, maybe she would master that fine art.

Reporters shouting questions dragged her back to the here and now.

"Hold your questions," McCabe ordered, raising his hands stop sign fashion. "Mr. Cole, Sylvia's father, has something to say first." McCabe surveyed the crowd. "Please, be respectful of how difficult this time is for these people. I'll answer all your questions to the best of my ability when Mr. Cole completes his statement."

McCabe stepped back from the podium and Zion Cole moved forward. Without his presence next to her, Yolanda sagged against Laney. Laney put an arm around her waist and held her steady.

Mr. Cole spoke of his beautiful daughter, of the light she had brought to their lives, of the immense contributions she had made to this community. He grasped the podium with both hands as if he needed it for leverage to remain vertical.

"My wife and I," he said, then hesitated to steady his voice, "are offering a one million dollar reward to anyone who provides information leading to the arrest of the person who brutally strangled our daughter. Someone saw or heard something. Please," he cried, "come forward. We want justice for our sweet Sylvia."

He turned away and moved back to his wife's side. Questions fired in the air once more. McCabe answered each one even if it was only to say we just don't have that information at this time.

"Please." Mrs. Cole turned to Laney. "I can't take anymore."

Laney ushered the parents into City Hall, away from the crowd and the ongoing discussions of their daughter's murder. As much as she wished Mr. Cole hadn't announced the cause of death, she wasn't about to mention the slip. He was in enough pain without being made to feel as if he'd made a misstep.

The police department spanned half the building. The other half housed the city planning office as well as the water and utility service departments. Water was about the only resource citizens in Shutter Lake had to worry about carving into their budgets. A number of the wealthy geniuses who called Shutter Lake home had decades ago pushed the town to the forefront of alternative energy sources. Shutter Lake operated completely by solar and thermal energy. Local taxes were a little higher than average but part of that revenue took care of maintenance for the forest of solar panels just outside the city limits, as well as the underground works that no one ever saw.

Today, other than the dispatcher and receptionist, City Hall was empty. All their resources were in the field or working crowd control outside. Laney nodded to the two women as she crossed the lobby, ushering the Coles down the hall and into her office. Both she and McCabe had offices. There was one big room further down the hall for the officers to share. Beyond their shared space was a conference room, small break room and then the locker room and bathrooms.

Some enterprising soul, maybe the receptionist or the dispatcher, had decorated for fall. Plump pumpkins likely picked up at the farmers' market sat on either side of the main entrance. Black cats and broomsticks along with pointy-hatted witches were taped in the windows. Rather than homey and friendly, the decorations seemed somber and out of place under the circumstances.

Laney pushed the best smile she could into place. "Can I get you some water or coffee?"

Mrs. Cole shook her head, her face buried in a handkerchief.

Mr. Cole studied the framed accolades hanging on the wall behind Laney's desk. "You worked homicide in Los Angeles."

It wasn't a question. Cole was on the City Council. He had seen Laney's resume. "Yes, sir. Seven years in the department, two as a homicide detective. Before becoming a police officer, I studied criminal justice at California State University."

"Your father was a cop, too. A homicide detective as well." Cole's gaze met hers then. "He died in the line of duty."

"That's right."

His eyes searched Laney's long enough to make her uneasy.

"Do you recognize a killer—a monster—when you see one, Deputy Chief Holt?"

His question should have surprised her but somehow it didn't. Cole was the sort of man accustomed to controlling his universe. His daughter's murder had sent that universe spiraling out of his control.

"What do *you* think a monster looks like, Mr. Cole?" She watched his face, noted the surprise that she dared to answer his question with a question of her own.

"I'm not sure I know anymore." He looked away. "There was a time when I thought everything was black and white but I know now that isn't true."

Feeling like a jerk for not simply answering his question, Laney offered, "There are monsters you recognize the moment you see them. The total nutjobs who can't control their impulses. The super creepy ones who think they're in control but you sense the evil emanating from them before they even move or open their mouths. But then, there are others."

His blue eyes narrowed. "Others?"

"The ones who look just like you and me. The ones you never see coming."

He closed his eyes and exhaled a breath of sheer exhaustion. "Find him for me, Deputy Holt." His gaze nailed hers once more. "You're the one who can do it."

"I'll do my best, sir. We all will."

He turned his attention to Mrs. Cole. "I'm taking my wife home now."

Mrs. Cole grabbed Laney's arm before her husband could usher her from the office. "When can we have our baby back? We…" She cleared her throat. "We need to plan the funeral."

"Soon, hopefully," Laney offered. "We'll know more tomorrow about the coroner's schedule. It's very important that we allow him as much time as he needs. He can be a great help to our investigation."

Mrs. Cole blinked then nodded. "Thank you."

Laney touched her arm. "There are a lot of details to sort out. I would think you could go ahead and make all the necessary arrangements while leaving the date pending."

The woman nodded, her lips struggling to lift into a smile. "Thank you. Yes. There's plenty I can do while we wait."

Laney showed the Coles out through the rear exit to where they had parked their car in the employee lot. She watched until they were out of view.

One thing Mr. Cole could count on was that if anyone

listening today had information the department would hear about it soon. A million dollars was a lot of money. The flipside to that was there would be no shortage of dead end calls as well.

The cell phone at Laney's waist vibrated. She pulled it free of its holster and checked the screen. McCabe.

Meet me at The Rabbit Hole.

The chief wanted her to meet him at his favorite pub. Laney sighed. She really wanted to go home. Take a nice long run, and then an extended shower to melt all the kinks in her muscles. She needed time to digest today's events. Oh well, at least it was after five. McCabe had contained his own needs all day. She had to give him grace, it couldn't have been easy. She typed in a response and hit send.

On my way.

The Rabbit Hole was off the town's center square, just barely. The place lived up to its name. The sidewalk in front was covered with green turf; iron streetlamps had been painstakingly crafted to look like trees with crooked, bare limbs. There were no windows. The exterior was painted black, all of it, top to bottom except for the white rabbit painted next to the entrance, which was also black. Since Halloween was swiftly approaching creepy spider webs and massive spiders had been added around the entrance. The holiday décor did nothing to make the place more inviting in Laney's opinion.

As she stepped inside, she did have to admit that the chief was smart to suggest coming as soon as the press conference was over. It was only six and already the place was buzzing. Booths and tables were crowded with patrons. Inside the walls and floor were black. One wall featured a particularly creepy mural of a scene from Alice in Wonderland. The dim lighting allowed for a semblance of privacy, the beer was cold and the staff was cheery but the best part of The Rabbit Hole was the food. From wings to pork rind oyster snacks everything served at The Rabbit Hole was unexpectedly good and designed to be eaten with your fingers.

No need to search for McCabe, he had his own booth in the farthest corner from the door, slightly beyond the west end of the bar. The chief didn't have to worry about anyone bumping into him because the only people who passed his special spot were staff. He sat on the side of the booth that allowed him to keep an eye on the door. A good cop never wanted to sit with his or her back to the door.

Laney slid into the other side, back to the door. She wasn't too worried. Until today, no one ever ended up murdered in Shutter Lake. Besides, she felt confident McCabe had her back. Despite his relationship with alcohol, he was a good cop.

"I ordered your usual."

A tall sweating glass of draft sat on the table along with a basket of sweet potato fries. The fries were a mainstay of her diet. The beer, not so much, unless she was keeping the chief company.

"Thanks." She dug into the fries first. Neither of them had taken time for lunch. Alcohol, even if only beer, was a bad thing on an empty stomach.

"A million dollars." McCabe shook his head. "Every lunatic in the tri-county area will be calling in. Hell, maybe in the tri-state area."

She reached for the beer. "Maybe we'll get lucky and one of them really will have seen or heard something. And you never know, sometimes killers like to brag."

He downed the last of the beer in his glass. Considering there was another empty one sitting on the table, he was down two already. Laney sipped hers slowly. One of them would have to do the driving and odds were it wouldn't be McCabe. She wondered again why the man felt compelled to drink himself into oblivion every night. Maybe one of these days he would share whatever part of his past haunted him. Not that she was in any hurry. Whenever people shared the ugliest parts of their histories, they inevitably expected a Kumbaya moment.

Maybe another day.

"Cole thinks you're the only hope we've got of solving her murder." McCabe's brown eyes locked with Laney's. "How do you feel about that, Holt?"

This from the man who only hours earlier asked her to be lead on the investigation because she had the experience. "The best hope we have of finding the truth is working together. Drawing on every resource in the community. That's how I feel. What about you, McCabe?"

He smiled, motioned for the bartender to bring him another. "Good answer, but the truth is, I think he's right. A smart man knows when he's bested."

"We'll need some temporary help to cover the hotline calls." They had touched on this briefly before the press conference when Cole brought up the reward. The phone lines would be blazing twenty-four/seven.

"I pulled in our auxiliary officers."

Laney nodded "I didn't think of that." The only time they'd called in the auxiliary officers was when the Weatherly grandchild had wandered off. Only five, it was the boy's first time staying with his grandparents without one or both his parents. After that nine-hour search, Laney doubted he would be visiting again anytime soon without a parent with him.

"They'll work twelve on, twelve off, rotating days. I

think between the four of them they can handle the call lines with no problem."

"Their training should help with sorting the priority of the calls." She picked up another fry. "Good move, Chief."

He held her gaze for a beat. "I want you to re-interview Sylvia's staff. This time talk to them alone. I'm not so sure the women opened up in front of me the way they will if it's just you."

Laney shrugged. "Sure. I can do that."

"Her mother's making a list of the people Sylvia was closest to. Zion said he'd give me a list of business associates—ones her staff might not be aware of. Apparently she was doing some investing. We should have those lists first thing in the morning."

"Maybe all those stacks of cash are from her investments," Laney speculated.

McCabe grunted. "Most of us keep a little petty cash lying around. Who knows, when you're from a family as rich as hers maybe that is petty cash."

Laney chuckled. "Maybe."

"I guess we should rule out drugs and prostitution."

Laney's eyebrows reared up. "I've only lived in Shutter Lake for two years but I'm relatively certain we don't have a rampant drug issue or an ongoing prostitution ring that would draw in that sort of cash."

He blew out a frustrated breath. "Yeah, I know. I'm grasping at straws here."

They both were. "On a more personal level, I'm surprised a young, beautiful woman like her didn't seem to have any romantic entanglements." Laney traced a bead of water down the side of her glass with her fingertip. "No matter how independent she was, she surely had needs."

Another couple of beats elapsed with McCabe staring at her. She didn't have to look up from the sweating glass.

She could feel his gaze probing long before he spoke. "What about you? You have needs, Holt?"

Laney leaned back in her seat, downed a slug of beer, before looking at him. "None I can't take care of myself."

He shook his head, laughed. "I guess I asked for that one."

The third beer went down the hatch. He ordered another.

"Well, maybe Sylvia Cole took care of her own needs, too," he said.

The attentive bartender arrived with another beer for McCabe and grabbed the glasses he'd emptied. "Another for you, Laney?"

"No thanks, Ray." Laney flashed him a smile.

Visibly disappointed, the bartender moved on.

Ray Jones was not just a bartender. He owned and operated this popular establishment. He was about Laney's age and far too easy on the eyes for comfort. Dark hair, even darker eyes, muscles testing the seams of his tight black tee and equally tight black jeans. But the man had trouble written all over his handsome body. His lady's man reputation was one of the first rumors Laney heard when she settled in Shutter Lake.

McCabe chuckled again. "You're giving that guy a complex. He's not used to being turned down by the ladies."

"He'll get over it." Laney turned up her beer again. She wondered if Sylvia Cole had gone down that partic-ular rabbit hole. Or had she turned down the handsome bartender, too?

CHAPTER FOUR

Connie Bradshaw stood at the kitchen sink staring out the window at the darkness of the night. The café lights hanging from the pergola swayed in the wind, winking at her.

Sylvia Cole was dead.

Murdered.

Good God, what had she done?

Connie's fingers tightened on the glass in her hand until a crack snapped her from the daze. Thank heavens it hadn't shattered. She tossed the fractured glass into the trash bin and struggled to slow her pounding heart.

She had told Vernon in no uncertain terms what she would do if he did not end his affair with that little bitch. She'd thought her troubles were over six months ago when she'd fired her cleaning service. But she'd been wrong.

Fury tightened her lips.

As much as she had despised the arrogant little bitch she hadn't expected him to kill her!

What would happen now? Would they lose everything? The pharmaceutical company. Their home. The nest egg they had been building since before Vinn, their son, was born—more money than that little whore could ever fathom.

Connie was glad she was dead.

She shook her head, tears burning her eyes. Surely Vernon wouldn't have gone that far. She thought of all the times they had fought, at how angry Vernon would become. On more than one occasion she'd been certain he wanted to hit her.

But he never had. Not once in their twenty-five years of marriage.

She did everything in her power to stay attractive. Kept those infernal gray roots touched up. She went to yoga class three times a week, and body pump workouts at least twice a week. Most of the time she ate like a bird, depriving herself of her favorite foods and even decent quantities of the healthy stuff.

How was it that her fifty-nine year old husband—a full four years older than her and bearing down on sixty—could stay lean and sexy without the slightest effort? It just wasn't fair.

No. Fury roared through her again. What wasn't fair was some young, skinny bitch throwing herself at an older married man just because she could. Connie knew it was wrong. She should be sad that Sylvia had been murdered. But she wasn't. She was glad the little bitch had gotten strangled to death. She would love to have wrapped her fingers around her long, graceful neck and personally choked the life out of her.

But what if it was Vernon?

As if her worries had summoned him, Vernon walked up onto the back deck, directly into her line of vision. He paused and tapped the ash from his favorite pipe. She blinked and busied herself with tucking the rest of the dinner dishes into the dishwasher.

Her husband came into the house, placed his pipe on the counter and moved up behind her. "Dinner was wonderful. You outdid yourself, sweetheart."

His arms went around her waist and he leaned into her backside, pressing himself intimately against her. She barely contained a shudder at the disgusting feel of him, at the toxic smell of tobacco. She had long ago forced him to take his bad habit outside.

Evidently her revulsion to his touch had given him the idea that taking his other habit outside their home was acceptable as well. Bastard.

She stiffened. "I'm glad you enjoyed it."

"Did you order the flowers for Zion and Yolanda?"

Connie froze. "Yes." It was a lie but he wouldn't know the difference. The Coles would receive dozens upon dozens of cards and flower arrangements. What was he going to do, walk up to them and ask if they'd received the one from the Bradshaws?

Hardly.

Feeling her withdrawal, he moved away and leaned against the counter. For half a minute he didn't say anything, just watched her. Then he asked, "Did you confront Sylvia the way you threatened?"

Renewed anger ignited inside her and she barely restrained lashing out at him. Vinn was in the house somewhere. She never wanted him to know what his father had done. Turning seventeen was difficult enough without learning that his father was a lying, cheating, womanizing bastard.

Connie took a deep breath and decided to be completely honest. She was sick to death of the secrets and the lies. "I did." She reached for a towel and dried her hands. "I paid her another visit yesterday." A hateful smile stretched across her lips. "I told her if she didn't stay away from my husband I would go to her father and tell him what a little whore she was." She tossed the towel back to the counter. "Believe it or not, she actually had the audacity to cry as if I'd offended her. I hope she was still crying when whoever killed her watched her take her last breath."

Vernon's face twisted in anger. "You loathsome bitch," he snarled.

Suddenly his body was pressing into hers again. He trapped her against the sink. She glared into his dark eyes and begged him with her own to raise his hand to her—to dare to slap her or worse. She would take him for all his damned billions. She would get half in any event.

Sometimes she wondered if he had ever dreamed of killing her. Her lips tightened with a new wave of fury. Just let him try.

"How dare you call me names when you're the one who cheated!" Connie gasped, reminded herself that their son was in the house. Dear God, she needed to pull herself together. None of this mattered anymore. The issue was dead. Literally.

And she was glad, by God. So damned glad.

"You care for no one but yourself," he growled, his usually calm and kind voice a low roar. "I told you I would handle it. I made my choice—our family over her. More importantly, what she and I shared meant nothing. It was purely physical."

Outrage pulled her lips into a sneer. She drew back as far from him as possible. "I suppose that's why I saw you in your study crying after the press conference."

"What kind of person wouldn't cry when a neighbor dies from such a shocking and violent death? She's Yolanda and Zion's daughter, for God's sake. I've known her since she was a child. Of course I cried."

"Did you think of the sweet little girl she once was when you were screwing her?"

Vernon recoiled as if she had slapped him. "You are heartless. Completely heartless."

"Why don't we tell our son what you did and share with him what I said and see who he thinks is heartless?"

"Leave Vinn out of this!"

"Leave me out of what?"

Vernon whirled toward the sound of their son's voice. Horrified, Connie scooted away from him.

"It's nothing, son." Vernon was the first to recover. "Your mother and I simply disagree on how to renovate the kitchen."

Vinn looked to Connie and somehow she mustered a smile. "I told him we would ask you to cast the deciding vote."

Vinn looked from Connie to his father and back. "I'm with you, Mom. Whatever you decide about the kitchen is probably best."

"Of course." Vernon covered the few steps between them and clapped Vinn on the back. "Why didn't I think of that?"

Connie silently prayed that her husband's little disgusting pipe tobacco indulgence would give him lung cancer and that he would die an agonizing death. Very soon.

She smiled. "You're such a smart son, Vinn."

CHAPTER FIVE

"I could drive myself home, you know."

Laney glanced at McCabe, gave him a fake smile. "That's what all drunks say."

He slumped in the seat and laughed. "Yeah, I guess they do."

At the next traffic signal she braked to a stop for the red light and considered her boss. His eyes were closed. It wasn't that late, only nine-thirty. That he was drifting off was another indication of his level of inebriation. He'd wanted to stay at The Rabbit Hole longer but she knew from experience where that would lead. He'd drink even more and if anyone said the wrong thing to him or simply said something he took the wrong way, he would make a fool of himself.

This didn't happen often, she told herself as the light turned green and she rolled forward. His drinking hadn't really been an issue before. Nothing ever happened that required both her attention as well as his at the same time. If he wasn't up to the task of being the cop in charge at night or early in the morning, she was always there. She hadn't taken a vacation or gone beyond Sacramento since she moved to Shutter Lake. Peace and quiet was what she needed and that had been right here.

Until today.

Now the peace and quiet was shattered. Now both she and McCabe needed to be sober and in the moment.

"We should talk about this."

As they left Main Street behind and headed to Salt Creek Road where McCabe lived, the dim glow from the dash was the only available light. His eyes remained closed in spite of her comment. She hoped he hadn't passed out.

He stirred in the seat and she shifted her attention back to the road. "Are you listening, Chief?"

"Sure. Why wouldn't I be?" He sat up straighter. "What do you want to talk about?"

"I've never liked anyone getting into my business," she admitted, "and I've never wanted to be one of those people who gets into other people's business."

He grunted, maybe in agreement, maybe just so she would think he was paying attention.

Laney tightened her fingers on the steering wheel and plunged on. "I enjoy our working relationship. God knows I appreciate how much you trust me to be in charge whenever you're—"

"What the hell, Laney?" He shifted in the seat to stare at her profile. "Have you been offered a position some place else? Sacramento, maybe? I thought you wanted small town. Laid back."

He wasn't making this easy. "No, Chief. I haven't been offered another job. Shutter Lake is exactly where I want to be." She slowed for a turn. "Under normal circumstances I have no issue with your drinking, but I need your full focus on this case. This murder has changed everything, at least temporarily. If you could just slow down a little until we sort this one out I would be a lot happier."

Silence thickened between them all the way to the man's driveway. Laney navigated the circular drive, pulling to a stop in front of his porch. She shifted into Park and cut the engine. McCabe's ranch style house stood on a rise overlooking the valley. He had a sizeable chunk of land and a couple of horses. Inside the house was nice, not fancy, more country style. No fuss, no pretense. Like the owner.

She really didn't want any hard feelings between them.

"Yeah, I know." He sat up straighter in his seat. "I've taken advantage of your flexibility ever since you got here. Knowing you had things under control made it easier for me to slip out of control."

"I'm not saying you're anything less than a good cop." Laney leaned against the headrest, turned her face toward him. "I have no problem with the way we usually work together. It's just that for now, I need—the department and the community need—your full attention whether I'm lead on the investigation or not. Whatever I do, people will be looking to you for assurances. You're the one they trust, the one they look up to. Not me."

He blew out a big breath. "You're right. I'll get my shit together and see you in the morning."

She relaxed a little. "We'll find the person who did this. If nothing else someone is going to want that million dollars."

McCabe shook his head. "Hell, I want it."

Laney laughed. "I'll pick you up in the morning since your Bronco is at the office. Seven work for you?"

He growled, ran a hand over his face. "Yeah, sure. Just bring the coffee."

"Will do."

Laney stayed until he was through the front door. Then she rolled down the drive and headed back to town. Beyers Lane, her street, was only a mile from Main Street but tonight it felt like it was a hundred miles. The trees, lots and lots of trees had drawn Laney to this house. A 1960's split level, the house was still as stuck in the decade as when she bought it. Not in bad shape, just out of style. So far she'd done some painting and pulled up the disagreeable carpet added in the 80's. The kitchen would need to be tackled eventually, but not anytime soon. Electrical and plumbing were above her pay grade.

Her headlights flashed over the barn red house as she rolled to a stop. "Home sweet home."

If she ever got around to cleaning out her garage she wouldn't have to park in the driveway and climb the front steps when she came home this late and this tired. How could a person still have unpacked boxes sitting around after two years?

Maybe because the parts of her old life that were still in those boxes were no longer relevant.

"Good point," she muttered.

Sliding the key into the front door lock she couldn't help wondering if she should get a security system. Who would have thought she'd need one here? Inside, she flipped on the light, tossed her keys on the table next to the door and locked up. Pearl meowed and trotted over to greet her. She was the one good thing from L.A. she'd brought to Shutter Lake with her. The cat had followed her around a crime scene at an old abandoned warehouse. Gray and dirty, her fur had been ratty and it was obvious she didn't get enough to eat.

Laney reached down and stroked her now silky fur. "Hey, girl. You been holding the fort down for me?"

Leaving her at that crime scene had been out of the

question. Her partner had thought she was out of her mind to take home a stray cat. Maybe she had been but she just couldn't leave the poor thing to starve to death. A visit to the vet and to the groomer and the cat turned out to be in reasonably good health and white instead of gray, thus the name Pearl.

Pearl liked the new house. Loads of room to roam and lots of big windows for watching the birds.

Laney put fresh water in her bowl and filled her food dish. She stretched and considered the time. She should shower and hit the sack, but her nerves were still jumping. She needed a run. A long one.

She hurried up the stairs to her bedroom and shed the trappings of work. Placed her service weapon and her badge in the drawer of the bedside table. Peeled off her jacket and the shirt. Then she toed off the shoes and dispensed with the trousers. She chose the heavier running clothes since it was cold outside. October nights often dropped to the low forties, like tonight.

Lastly she tucked her blond hair into a beanie, strapped the carrier for her cell phone and her pepper spray around her upper left arm and tucked her personal handgun into her waistband at the small of her back. Despite the murder sending shock waves through the community, she wasn't actually concerned about her safety running in Shutter Lake, even at night. The wildlife was a different story. To them, she was the intruder, the safety concern. Everything from raccoons to mountain lions, and the latter wasn't exactly put off by a badge.

"I'll be back, Pearl," Laney called as she slipped out the front door. She locked it and placed the single key into its compartment in the armband carrier. A few minutes of warm up stretches and she was off.

She drew the brisk night air deep into her lungs and allowed her mind to zero in on the investigation. Point by point she reviewed the findings at the crime scene. The perp who murdered Sylvia Cole was without doubt someone the victim knew. Whether or not it was the same person with whom she'd recently had sex was the most immediate question they needed to answer. No one seemed to know about a boyfriend. It wasn't such a surprise that the parents weren't up to speed on Sylvia's love life but it was odd that Fernandez wasn't. The two had been friends and colleagues for years.

Then there was the cash. Laney and McCabe hadn't yet dug into that development. Way more cash than anyone should have lying around, particularly if her only means of support was her business. Of course she could have gotten the money from her parents. They certainly had plenty. But why keep it in a safe, an unlocked one at that? Why wouldn't she want her nest egg drawing interest?

There were usually only two reasons for folks to keep large sums of money in a home safe: they wanted to have some amount of cash handy for emergencies or they were hiding it from the IRS. This was way more money than anyone would need to have on hand for an emergency, in Laney's opinion.

Since when was two hundred and sixty thousand dollars petty cash?

Whatever Sylvia Cole was involved with, whether it was legal or not, her murder was likely somehow related to the cash.

But why didn't her killer take the money?

The safe was unlocked. He could have bagged it and the cops would never have been the wiser. Fernandez certainly had the opportunity to take it. If the second in command at Sparkle didn't know about the cash in her boss's safe then it probably wasn't related to the business.

During the next interview of the parents, that question would be asked. For now, the banded bundles of cash were being checked for prints. The bed sheets had gone to the lab. The extra toothbrush found in a drawer in the bathroom was off to the lab, too. The hair in the brush, as well as dozens of other items were carefully collected. Tomorrow Laney would interview the employees again. The list of the victim's friends Yolanda Cole was preparing would no doubt be long. Everyone in Shutter Lake knew everyone else. The lists would need to be prioritized by those closest to the victim and to her family. Ana Perez, the town's only doctor, would be high on that list. She and Sylvia were close friends. At least, they appeared to be. Laney hadn't talked to Ana yet but she'd seen the two out together on numerous occasions. Laney considered Ana a friend as well, but Ana was very private with her friendships just as she was with her patients. No matter that Ana, Julia, Laney and Dana Perkins, the school principal, were friends and enjoyed a regular girls' night out fairly frequently, they all four kept their secrets. The bond between them was a solid one, but, Laney supposed, they all had their reasons for not going beyond a certain point. Each one of them had a history with pieces they apparently didn't want to share. This aspect might have bugged Laney's natural instinct to investigate, except she had secrets of her own as well.

Some secrets were best left in the past.

Dismissing the thought, the sound of her shoes on the pavement echoed in the darkness, bringing her attention back into focus on the here and now. Not too dark tonight. A big old full moon glowed mournfully. Her heart rate climbed, her respiration rate matching it. She ran almost every night. A little over a mile to town, around the center and a few select side streets, and then a mile back. About five miles. Not so much. There was a time when she'd run twice that much or more.

But she'd been running from her demons back then.

Still did, really. There wasn't a night that passed that she didn't see that young boy's face at least once before she drifted off to sleep. She pushed forward. Running faster.

Twelve years old, he'd taken the gun from his older brother's bedroom. The older brother had been a straight up thug. Still, the kid looked up to him, wanted to be just like him. So he'd taken the gun, gotten on his bicycle and rode around until he found some trouble to get into. He hadn't realized the cops were marking off a homicide scene just across the way. He'd parked his bike and thought he'd have a closer look. It was late, dusk had fallen. The time of night when the fading light and the encroaching gloom played tricks on your eyes.

No one would ever know why he took that shot, hit her partner in the right shoulder. Laney had chased the shooter. Hadn't realized he was a kid. He'd been tall for his age. When he rounded that corner and turned back to fire his weapon again, she had no option. It was him or her. He'd already shot her partner.

She had taken the shot.

The bullet hit its mark and he was dead.

Twelve years old.

That moment when she rolled him onto his back and realized she'd just shot and killed a child would haunt her for the rest of her life. No matter that Internal Affairs had cleared her of wrongdoing. No matter that the department had protected her when the press tried to make her the guilty party. All the counseling in the world would never enable her to forgive herself. She would never get over what she did that day.

She never wanted to be in that position again.

Never.

But she was a cop. Being a cop was more than a job, it was who she was. So she did the only thing she could. She found the most sedate small town possible where she could live and still be a cop without the fear of ever killing someone else's child.

Shutter Lake was the epitome of small, tranquil, clean living. Farmers in the area had taken organic farming to the next level. Most of the pubs brewed their own beer. From the bakery to the coffee shop and everything in between, folks prided themselves on clean and healthy and just plain good. The school was a private entity, bestowed with a prestigious blue ribbon every year. Even the good doctor, Ana Perez, operated a wellness center three nights a week in the community gathering hall. Healthiness was a lifestyle for most residents.

Then there was the chief. Laney had almost asked him on a couple of occasions why he felt the need to drink himself into oblivion most nights. He had been married once, she knew. She'd heard that his wife had left him. Whatever happened, he hadn't married again. Not that forty was so old, but she got the distinct impression he wasn't interested in long term.

Something he had in common with the victim.

According to everyone interviewed so far, Sylvia Cole liked her independence and maybe she had. Yet, based on all that cash in her home she certainly had at least one secret.

There was always the possibility someone passing through had murdered her. Some transient who had hoped for a little help from a Good Samaritan. It's possible she'd opened the door with the intention of giving him some cash. Maybe the situation turned confrontational and he felt compelled to kill her.

Laney dismissed the theory. It just didn't fit. Sylvia had opened the door to her killer. She'd been dressed in nothing but a nightshirt at the time. A woman at home alone dressed so scantily wouldn't have opened the door to a stranger. Not a savvy businesswoman like Sylvia Cole. A woman who had traveled extensively. Though she had grown up in Shutter Lake she had been well aware of the world around her.

Laney slowed as she reached the final stretch of Main Street. A lone figure huddled on the bench outside The Grind. Male, she decided as she grew closer. A paper sack molded to the shape of a bottle sat between his feet.

She slowed to a walk, let her respiration even out. When she was nearly even with his position, she said, "Full moon tonight."

The man's head shot up and Laney's hand went instinctively to the small of her back.

He shivered as if he'd only just realized how cold it was. He wasn't wearing a coat. Only a black tee sporting The Grind logo and equally dark jeans.

Nolan Ikard, the owner.

"Yeah, it's a bright one." He cleared his throat and glanced up at the moon as if he hadn't noticed until that moment.

Whether it was the cold or whatever was in the bottle, his speech was a little slurred.

"You okay?" She stopped next to the bench, stretched her back.

"Sure. Just thinking." He reached for the paper sack, downed a slug of whatever was in the bottle.

She said, "everyone's shook up over Sylvia's murder."

His head jerked up again, his gaze met hers. "It's…It's hard to believe. She…"

When he didn't say more, she asked, "Did you know her well?"

His sandy blond hair looked disheveled, as if he'd been running his fingers through it over and over. He shrugged. "Yeah. Pretty well. We were…we were friends."

Laney considered his age and asked, "Did you go to school with her?"

He nodded, his fingers tightening around the sack, making it crinkle. "I used to pull her pigtails when we were kids. She pretended to hate it, but I think she liked it."

Laney doubted Dana was old enough to have been the principal there when Sylvia and Nolan attended.

Curious, Laney sat down on the bench next to him. The scent of freshly ground coffee beans lingered on his clothes, probably on his skin, too. "Do you know if she was involved with anyone? Maybe a boyfriend she didn't want her parents to know about?"

He shook his head. "Sylvia didn't have a boyfriend. She liked being free. You know." He looked at Laney and smiled sadly. "She was just enjoying life and being herself."

Laney thought about that for a bit. "Everybody needs somebody sometime."

"Wait." He laughed, the sound broken and hoarse. Definitely drunk. "I know that song. That old guy sung it. Everybody needs somebody…," he crooned.

The off-key lyrics drifted off.

"Is there anything about Sylvia you'd like to tell me, Nolan?" He seemed more upset than a mere old school mate who felt sad about the loss.

He shook his head. "No. She…she was happy. And smart." He smiled. "Really smart. Way smarter than anyone knew." He exhaled a big breath permeated with the scent of whiskey. "I don't know why anyone would want to kill her."

"That's what we're going to find out." Laney stood. "Let's get you home before you freeze." He lived on the second floor of the coffee shop. The stairs were in the alley between The Grind and Batter Up Bakery. "I need you making coffee bright and early in the morning."

He got to his feet. Swayed. "Don't worry. I've never opened late before."

Laney walked him down the alley and guided him up the iron stairs. It took him a couple of tries to get the key into the lock.

Once he had the door open, she ordered, "lock the door behind you."

He nodded. "Thanks. G'night, Deputy."

"Goodnight, coffee guy."

He laughed another of those shattered sounds and closed the door.

Laney waited until she heard the lock engage before she headed back down the stairs. Whether he knew it or not, Nolan Ikard had just made his way onto her persons of interest list.

"The list that won't end," she muttered

She broke into a sprint, headed for home.

Tomorrow was going to be a long day.

CHAPTER SIX

Friday, October 5

Laney inhaled the dark, decadent aroma of coffee. At quarter to seven in the morning that scent was exactly what she needed. The bell over the door jingled as it closed behind her. Two lines of customers were cued up to the counter at The Grind.

It was the same every morning, even Sundays. She took her place in the longer of the two lines. And why wouldn't the one and only coffee shop in a town that offered an endless variety of delectable coffees and exotic teas be busy? One of the pubs served breakfast and two of the three restaurants in town did, as well. But no one had coffee like The Grind. Not to mention the bagels and croissants were excellent.

Next door, Heidi Udall frequently threatened to open up her bakery, Batter Up, for coffee and sugary treats, but so far it was only talk. Udall probably brought up the

subject now and again just to scare her Main Street neighbor. If Nolan Ikard, barista and entrepreneur, was ever
found murdered, Udall would be at the top of Laney's
suspect list. The woman's personality could be grating at
times, but she made a mean almond flavored cupcake with
butter cream icing. She thought of the box of cupcakes in
the victim's fridge. It was a shame to let them go to waste.

Can't eat the evidence, Laney.

The crowd of customers had disappeared by the time it
was her turn—which was the point of choosing the longest
line. Based on her experience, by seven fifteen or twenty
there would be another rush so she didn't have a lot of
time. For the past six or so minutes she had watched Nolan
and the other barista, Shonda Reed, put on a show with
their coffee making groove and their flirty personalities.
Both were young, attractive, under thirty for sure.

As Laney bellied up to the counter Nolan's attention
landed on her and his expression immediately closed. The
playful, carefree attitude vanished as quickly as if she'd
tossed cold water on him. "G'morning, Deputy Holt. What
can I get for you?"

"I'll take two Red Eyes." Laney had a feeling McCabe
would need the extra caffeine. She could use the additional
blast as well.

"That'll definitely kick start your morning."

As he prepared the espresso shots for the coffees Laney
had ordered Nolan was strangely quiet. Shonda busied
herself with cleaning up and restocking before the next
rush. If not for the snappy music strumming from the
speakers, the place would have been as quiet as a stuffy
library. Laney studied Nolan. She stopped in The Grind
every morning except Sundays. It really was unlike him to
be so quiet and soberly focused. Maybe he was embarrassed about last night.

"Red Eyes have helped me through a hangover or two," she said, just to see his reaction.

He glanced up, managed to produce a ghost of a smile. "Works every time."

With those three words he went silent again. Laney watched his hands as he prepared the coffees, adding the espresso, then popping on the tops. His usually rhythmic movements were a little stilted, a little shaky. Not embarrassed, she decided. Nervous. What did Nolan have to be nervous about?

"No bagel this morning?" He placed the coffees in front of her and once more mustered up the smile that wasn't really a smile.

"Oh yeah. Got to have a bagel." She surveyed the array of goodies behind the glass. "I think I'll go with the sun-dried tomato. Two, please." She went back and forth on this morning's offerings of homemade cream cheese blends. Couldn't decide which one sounded the best. Her stomach grumbled, urging her to get on with it. "And some cucumber herb cream cheese." Otherwise she doubted McCabe would bother with food this morning.

Nolan bagged the rest of the order and gave her the total. His hand visibly shook when he accepted her debit card.

"You and Sylvia were close, huh?"

He glanced at her, surprise and uncertainty in his eyes.

Laney could envision the two together. Both were attractive. About the same age. Entrepreneurs. They had a lot in common. If Nolan was the one who left tracks on her sheets, did he know about Sylvia's other money—the stacks and stacks in the safe?

"I don't know what you mean." He passed the card, along with the receipt, back to her. "I knew her. Everybody did. I guess you could say we were friends. Went to school together and all."

Last night his memory of the victim had been a little different. Of course, alcohol had a way of loosening the tongue and amplifying the emotions. "We're looking for a boyfriend. Someone who might have been intimate with her."

The crash of stainless steel against stainless steel shattered the bubble of tension and made them both glance in Shonda's direction.

"Sorry." Her face reddened as she picked up the frothing pitchers scattered across the counter between the brewers and the dispensers.

Nolan's attention shifted back to Laney. "Like I told you, if Sylvia had a boyfriend I didn't know anything about it."

Laney noted that Shonda glanced back over her shoulder at him before she disappeared through the swinging door behind the counter. A follow up with the younger barista was in order. She clearly thought Nolan knew more than he was saying. That maybe he was more intimate with the victim than he wanted Laney to know.

His behavior last night was more telling than he likely realized.

Tucking her debit card away, Laney felt compelled to add, "We're not suggesting the boyfriend—or lover—is her murderer. All we need is any info he might be able to provide about her recent activities."

He shrugged, his eyes on the door as if anticipating the next customer. "Like I said, we were friends. Back in school, mostly." He looked directly at Laney then. "Anyone who knew her would be upset. Jesus, she was murdered. Does being upset or sad make me a suspect?"

"Absolutely not." Laney frowned to ensure he understood she felt his reaction was a bit over the top. "But you understand that we have to do everything possible to find her killer, don't you? Anyone who was her friend should want to help. The slightest bit of seemingly irrelevant information could make all the difference."

His expression shifted to defeat. She'd made her point. Laney liked Nolan. It wasn't her intent to make him more miserable, but she needed him to be honest.

"I wish I could help." His voice cracked and he cleared his throat. "Thanks for choosing The Grind. Have a good day."

The bell over the door jingled and he looked beyond Laney to greet the new customer. Relief brightened his expression. His exit strategy from this uncomfortable situation strolled up to the counter.

Laney took one last lingering look at him before leaving the shop. She would be talking to Nolan again. But before she did, she intended to see what Shonda knew about his relationship with the victim.

The new Shutter Lake Medical Clinic had been built right on the edge of town, just across the street from the Chamber of Commerce. The sprawling, one story stucco and brick building sat against a backdrop of towering trees. A wide, welcoming porch complete with rocking chairs fronted the entrance. Great care had been taken with the landscape of the parking area as well. Inside, the lobby was filled with comfortable chairs and current magazines. Every member of staff was friendly and accommodating.

Laney appreciated all those things but it was the doctor and nurses, the insanely well-equipped facility that really made her happy. With the City Council comprised of mostly older, wealthy people, money had been no object when it came to the design and execution of this new facility. Dr. Ana Perez had the very best equipment money could buy. From the hemostats to the imaging department and everything in between, only the most cutting edge would do. Laney had seen big city ERs far less ready for emergencies than this clinic. A half dozen nurses and two nurse practitioners ensured no one waited too long.

Though the clinic had a lobby full of patients, Perez took the time to see Laney and the chief in her office, away from the patients and the rest of the staff.

"We know you're busy," McCabe said, kicking off the interview, "we'll try to make our questions as direct and brief as possible."

Ana's long dark hair was captured in a ponytail. Like Laney, she preferred it out of the way. Laney wore hers in a ponytail most of the time. It was just easier. Not to mention for her it helped with the whole dumb blond stigma.

"I'm happy to help any way that I can," Ana assured the chief. She glanced at Laney. "Sylvia and I were friends. Good friends. We have been since she volunteered to represent the small businesses of Shutter Lake with the Chamber of Commerce. She was very passionate about the community. So many young people can't wait to grow up and leave home—particularly if home is a small town —but not Sylvia. She loved her life in Shutter Lake."

"She helped with your wellness classes," Laney said. She'd been to yoga a few times—not nearly as often as she should. Ana was always after her to attend more often. Sylvia had led one of the high-energy cardio programs. Laney preferred to get her cardio workout pounding the pavement.

"She did." Ana smiled sadly. "Everyone loved her. Her enthusiasm for fitness was contagious among all ages."

"Did Sylvia have any health problems that you're aware of?" McCabe asked.

Ana shook her head. "None. She was very healthy. After I heard," her voice trembled, "what happened, I checked her file just to be sure. She was always very healthy."

"No depression or anxiety?" Laney asked. "It's tough to be free of one or both in today's rush-rush world."

"Sylvia refused to watch the news," Ana explained. "She preferred to focus on her world, the one where she lived, in hopes of making it a better place."

Laney didn't miss the hint of worry that colored her older friend's tone as she said this. "Can you tell us about some of her efforts to make Shutter Lake a better place?"

Ana stalled, that deer caught in the headlights expression flashing for an instant. "Well, you're aware she served the Chamber of Commerce and that she volunteered at my wellness center."

Laney waited for more. Ana shifted in her chair. Tension elbowed its way into the room, pushing out far too much oxygen. Why was she so nervous? This was not like the steady doctor.

McCabe outmaneuvered the tension by moving on to another question. "Are you aware of any sort of trouble Sylvia might have been having with anyone?"

Ana shook her head instantly, adamantly.

"And yet she's dead," Laney pointed out, "murdered. Someone clearly was upset with her over something she had said or done."

Ana braced her forearms on her desk and stared at her hands for a moment before meeting Laney's gaze. "Sylvia and I were close, but we didn't share all our secrets. Who of us does?"

Laney had to give her that one.

"So, she did have secrets?" McCabe pressed.

The doctor flinched. "Doesn't everyone?"

"But not everyone ends up dead on her living room floor," Laney countered, framing the statement for the most shock value. She hated to use this sort of pressure on a friend, but she needed her to drop her guard. "We can't find Sylvia's killer if we don't know what was going on in her life. If you know anything—if you even suspect something that might help us please tell us, Ana—Dr. Perez. Any little thing could make all the difference."

Ana held up her hands. "All right, all right." She exhaled a resigned sigh. "I didn't want to bring this up, but on two occasions in the past week or so I saw Vinn Bradshaw talking to Sylvia in the parking lot after class at the gathering hall. He seemed upset and Sylvia appeared to be trying to calm him down. Whatever was up between them, it looked intense."

Vinn Bradshaw. He was a senior at the school. Quiet kid. Never been in any trouble as far as Laney was aware. She glanced at McCabe who looked as surprised as she felt. Laney asked, "Did Sylvia mention what was going on with Vinn?"

"She told me he had a crush on her and she was trying to let him down easy."

A warning throbbed through Laney. "Are you aware of any mental health or drug issues with Vinn?"

Ana shook her head. "You know I can't answer a question like that." She turned to McCabe. "If Vinn had a drug problem or a mental health issue with a propensity toward violence, wouldn't you know about that, Chief?"

"I'll take that as a no," Laney answered the question before McCabe said a word. She supposed that was as close as Ana could come to answering without breaking patient-doctor confidentiality.

"Do you have any other questions?" Ana appeared agitated now.

McCabe stood and extended his hand. "Thank you, Dr. Perez, you've been very helpful and we appreciate your time. We know how busy you are. It's possible we'll have other questions before this is done."

Laney was on her feet thrusting her hand across the desk right behind the chief's. "We only want to find the person who did this. This isn't about digging up dirt or sullying Sylvia's name."

It was best not to leave on a sour note which was the reason Laney felt compelled to explain the questions. If there was any hope of Ana coming to them with additional information, she had to feel comfortable with how they planned to use the parts that might seem negative.

Ana nodded. "I understand. I do. This is just such a tragedy. It's difficult to look at it from an objective place."

"Please," Laney urged, "if you think of anything at all that might help, call me. You have my number."

Like McCabe, Laney kept quiet until they were outside the clinic and well across the parking lot. "You know we can't go to the school and question the Bradshaw boy."

They stared at each other across the top of her vehicle.

"We can if one of the parents is willing to allow it," he countered.

Laney made a yeah-right face. "And which one of the parents is going to allow us to speak to their minor son about his potential involvement in a murder investigation without a lawyer present?"

"You let me worry about that part."

Couldn't hurt to try. The lists the Coles had provided this morning gave them no additional leads. A break would be good about now.

By noon they were waiting in a small conference room at Shutter Lake School. Dana, the principal, had arranged for Vinn to skip his college prep class. She smiled and said a young man as super intelligent as Vinn didn't really need it anyway. Vernon Bradshaw sat at the table, conversing casually with the chief as if his son wasn't about to be questioned in an ongoing murder investigation.

Laney was dying to know what McCabe had on the guy. Why would any father allow his son to be questioned in regards to a homicide without an attorney present?

Maybe one thoroughly convinced he had nothing to worry about?

Never a smart move either way, which suggested this intelligent man, who was the brains behind numerous internationally renowned pharmaceutical breakthroughs, owed McCabe something.

Just another one of those small town secrets.

Before coming to the school they'd had to stop by City Hall for a meeting with the mayor. Mayor Thomas Jessup wanted an update on the case. His office had been inundated with calls. When they finally left City Hall McCabe insisted on driving. Any time they worked together, he preferred to drive. Laney was only too happy to let him— as long as he wasn't hungover. In her opinion, a hungover driver was about as bad as a buzzed driver.

Dana arrived with Vinn. She smiled at those assembled and ushered the boy toward the remaining empty chair at the table. Every time Laney saw the principal she was smiling. She couldn't imagine how Dana spent her days surrounded by just over three hundred students and still keep that smile on her face. Not true. Laney knew. The woman loved the kids. She loved her job.

Dana glanced around the table. "Anyone need anything? Water? Coffee?"

Laney shook her head, the others declined as well.

"Well, then, just let me know if there's anything else I can do."

Dana exited, closing the door behind her.

Vinn Bradshaw was seventeen, tall—basketball player tall—lanky but handsome, and, like the principal, always smiling. Even now, when he was obviously nervous, his lips seemed to curl up into a smile. His pleasant expression was far more like his mom's than his dad's. Vernon Bradshaw had dark hair, too, but his was peppered with gray. His eyes were dark, not hazel like his son's. Vinn had the classic square jaw while Vernon had more of a long face with a sort of pointy chin that he kept covered with a well-manicured beard. The ends of his mustache connected to the beard, framing his thin lips. The man, late fifties, had that I'm-too-important-to-be-bothered air about him.

And yet he came running when McCabe called.

Interesting.

"We're all present, Chief," Vernon Bradshaw said, "why don't you tell us what this is about?"

"It's about Sylvia, of course," Vinn said sharply, his glare aimed at his father. "She's dead. Somebody murdered her."

Vinn had never struck Laney as the angry type. The kid always looked happy. Well, he was certainly angry now. "It is about Sylvia," Laney said to Vinn. "We really appreciate you talking to us, Vinn."

His father practically rolled his eyes. "My son barely knew her, why would you have questions for him?"

McCabe propped his elbows on the table and folded his arms. He stared directly at the elder Bradshaw for a beat before shifting his attention to Vinn. "Son, is it true that you and Sylvia had cross words a couple of times recently in the parking lot of the gathering hall?"

"Don't be ridiculous," Bradshaw said.

"Yes, sir." Vinn's face had gone pale.

Bradshaw lifted an eyebrow. "When did this happen?" The question was aimed at his son, no small amount of surprise packed into the four words.

Parents most always made this situation more difficult, but there was no getting around the man's presence. "No one is accusing you of anything, Vinn," Laney hastened to explain. "We're only looking for any trouble Sylvia may have been having. We thought you might know since you seemed upset on the occasions mentioned. Maybe you were trying to help—to give her advice—and she wouldn't listen."

McCabe's eyes practically high-fived Laney's for coming up with such a good and reasonable excuse for their questions.

Most boys Vinn's age wanted to feel like heroes, protectors. She doubted Vinn was any different. He was likely ready to be his own man. Rescuing a damsel in distress was a real life fantasy. Laney wanted to tap into that ego torrent.

Vinn kept his focus on Laney, his fingers gripping the edge of the table as if he feared he might suddenly jump up and run out of the room. "I liked Sylvia," he said, his voice a little shaky. "We were friends."

Laney expected him to be nervous, afraid even. This was tragic, scary business. "I'm certain she was fond of you as well, Vinn. I've heard nothing but great things about you. Ms. Perkins says you're planning to pursue a career in nanotechnology."

Vinn nodded. "I want to help develop better drug delivery systems. It's an exciting field."

"Wow. I can't even imagine." Laney shook her head.

"I'm glad we have students like you to take up the slack of folks like me."

A flush crept across his face and that ever present smile widened a bit. "Thanks. I'm lucky to have the opportunity."

"Why did you and Sylvia argue?" Laney nudged, maneuvering the conversation back to the reason for this impromptu interview. "Was she in trouble?"

He stared at the table, lifted his skinny shoulders in a shrug. "I don't know. She never said she was in trouble. We weren't in a good place the past few weeks."

"Did you have a crush on her?"

His head shot up, his gaze collided with Laney's. "No way! She was..." A note of anger infused the words. He took a breath, visibly calmed himself. "She was way too old for me."

"Friends argue sometimes," Laney suggested. "Any relationship has ups and downs. What were you and Sylvia arguing about?"

He lowered his face again, avoiding all eye contact. "I wanted her to stay out of *my* business."

"Was Sylvia harassing you somehow?" McCabe asked.

Vernon Bradshaw shook his head. "This is ridiculous. Of course she wasn't harassing him. Like I said, they barely knew each other."

"I knew enough," Vinn snarled at his father. "More than you think."

Laney and McCabe exchanged a look. The kid definitely had an underlying animosity related to the victim. That animosity appeared to spill over to his father. Not necessarily an unusual situation between teenagers and parents.

"What do you know, Vinn?" Laney asked quietly.

He shrugged again, looked anywhere but at her. "That

she lied about things and that's why we couldn't be friends anymore."

"What things?" McCabe pressed.

"This is nothing but a fishing expedition," Bradshaw complained, his tone dismissive.

"What did Sylvia lie about?" McCabe repeated, rephrasing the question.

"I don't know all the things exactly." Vinn glared at his father as if he had asked the question. "Stuff." He looked to McCabe then. "Just stuff."

"Vinn," Laney tried another route, "sometimes people make mistakes. Sylvia may not have meant to get into your business or to lie. Everybody says she was a nice person. We've done over a dozen of these interviews and people can't say enough nice things about her. I'll bet she apologized for whatever she did when you confronted her."

He looked directly at Laney then. "She didn't apologize. She wasn't sorry. She told me to grow up. She wasn't as nice as you or anyone else thinks. I guess I made a mistake liking her. Maybe somebody else did, too. Maybe that's why she's dead."

Bradshaw pushed his chair back and stood. "That's enough. We're done here." He grabbed his son by the arm to usher him to his feet. Vinn pulled away from his touch. "If you have any more questions for my son, you can direct them to our attorney."

Vinn stalked out of the room, his father right behind him.

McCabe hummed a note of surprise. "That was interesting."

Laney nodded. "Something Sylvia did or said really upset the kid."

Vinn Bradshaw had no record of trouble or any sort of violence. He was the quintessential good kid. Perfect attendance, perfect grades, amazing athlete, volunteered for all the right activities. Laney had a feeling his behavior during the interview was not typical at all. The question was, why?

"I guess Sylvia had at least one enemy after all." McCabe stood and pushed in his chair. "I didn't expect the one we finally unearthed to be a high school kid."

"You think he was involved with her physically?" Laney hoped that wasn't the case. She didn't want to believe a kid like Vinn would resort to murder, but it happened. Those dark images and sounds from the past whispered through her head. She forced them away. Not going back there.

"Are you kidding?" McCabe laughed. "Trust me, if he had the chance, he was. Sylvia Cole was gorgeous, any teenage boy would give his right nut for a chance to be with her."

Laney walked right into that one. "Yeah, yeah. I get it. Dumb question. *If* they were involved, maybe she realized her mistake—getting involved with a minor—and tried to break it off and he wasn't ready to walk away."

"Guys have killed for less."

She understood that primeval, animalistic instinct better than most.

Laney started to push in her chair, but hesitated. "Since the Bradshaws have lawyered up, if we want Vinn's prints we should get them now." She nodded toward the side of the table where Vinn had sat. "I imagine you can probably handle that, Chief."

"I'll get the kit from my Bronco." He started for the door but glanced back over his shoulder. "Another good reason for taking my vehicle. I'm always prepared."

Laney decided not to mention that she had a good stock of supplies, including a fingerprint kit, in her vehicle as well.

California was one of the states that required fingerprints for driver's licenses but sometimes it was just easier to do the collection on site. Cut down on the red tape.

When the chief was gone, she mulled over all that Vinn had said. Maybe lust had gotten the better of him. Even well behaved, smart guys like Vinn could fall victim to temptation. Once certain lines are crossed, everything changes. Leverage shifts and the best person can end up pressed into a corner. Fear and desperation prompted extreme reactions once cornered. Vinn Bradshaw had big plans for his future. It was possible Sylvia somehow threw a stumbling block in the way of those plans. If his parents had discovered something between their son and this young woman, all hell had probably broken loose. That could explain the hostility between father and son.

No, Laney decided. Vernon Bradshaw had too easily agreed to the interview. If he'd had something to fear, he would never have capitulated so readily. Then again, McCabe might have his own leverage. She shook her head. Still, most parents were far too protective to throw their own kids under the bus to save themselves.

Vinn's reaction was likely as big of a surprise to his father as it had been to Laney. He had not seen that coming.

Could Sylvia's murder be as simple as a teenage obsession?

Doubtful. For one thing, murder was rarely simple. And for another, there was all that cash. The array of theories on how the victim ended up with that kind of money in her house kept nagging at Laney. Her gut said Sylvia's murder was about more than a disagreement with a kid or a wad of plastic and cash from her purse.

There had to be more they were missing.

A lot more.

CHAPTER SEVEN

Laney grabbed a burger before going to the cleaning service office. Sparkle was on the east side of the down-town center. Shutter Lake was hardly more than sixty years old but the town had been designed with a vintage feel. Shops ranged in design from Victorian to Craftsman. Side-walks and streets were cobblestone. Green spaces heavily dotted the landscape. By the middle of September the fall décor had started to appear around town with lots of carved pumpkins and even a fake Jack O'Lantern here and there. Beginning in October, ghosts, black cats, witches and broomsticks had been added. In a few short weeks kids would be running around in costume for the fall festivities, including trick or treating.

Laney wasn't a big fan of holidays. Her time was better spent focused on work.

The Sparkle façade was Victorian with lots of pink details. Very feminine. Inside, the lobby was more like a parlor with lots of velvet and fringe. Laney had called Renata Fernandez and let her know that she needed to interview the employees again. She promised to make it as quick and as painless as possible so they could get back to their scheduled workday.

Renata complied without hesitation. She met Laney in the lobby. "Everyone's waiting in the conference room."

Laney nodded. "I appreciate you pulling the staff together for lunch. I'm sure it wasn't easy with their busy schedules."

"It was no problem," she explained as she led the way across the white-tiled lobby, "we generally meet here for lunch. Sylvie liked to ensure everyone had a good meal and a little time to rest. It was important to her to take care of her girls."

Sylvia sounded like a dream boss. Renata had also provided the company's records for all employees—for the second time. Laney noted they were paid well. All but one had been with Sylvia practically since she hired her first employee. There was only one former employee listed. One Josie Rodriguez who had stayed only three months and then left. There hadn't been an explanation listed in her file. Laney would ask about that later. Rodriguez's file hadn't been among the ones provided yesterday, just a note mentioning her brief employment.

Beyond the lobby there were two offices. The one with the lights turned off and the door closed was Sylvia's. Bundles of fresh flowers lay against the door. She was missed. Across the hall was Renata's office. Laney had reviewed the employee files in that office. Moving along the corridor they passed a bathroom. The final door on the left was the conference room/breakroom. At the end of the hall was the door to the storage room where cleaning supplies lined the shelved walls from floor to ceiling. The alley was accessed from that big room, as well. A small parking area directly behind the building was for employees. Six electric cars lined the parking area, each sporting the pink Sparkle logo.

At the door to the breakroom, Renata hesitated. "You may use my office again if you'd like to conduct each interview privately. For now we prefer to leave Sylvie's just as it was when she was last here."

"Thank you. Privacy would be good."

Laney started with Lucinda "Lucy" Gomez. Besides Renata, she had known Sylvia the longest. Gomez had grown up and still lived in nearby Grass Valley. She was twenty-five, petite with dark hair and eyes. Like all of Sylvia's employees, she was attractive and smart.

"Have you had a chance to think about the questions Chief McCabe and I asked you yesterday?" During yesterday's interviews the employees had been so upset that getting answers hadn't been easy. All the more reason to go over many of those same questions.

Lucy nodded. "I have thought about nothing else." She dabbed at her eyes with a wadded tissue. "I don't understand how anyone could hurt Sylvie. She was such a kind, giving person. You just don't know how much she did for all of us. She provides health insurance and I know that costs a lot. Our pay is way higher than average. Sylvie was always thinking of our best interests."

Although Laney appreciated the woman's loyalty, these were all things each of them had stated very distinctly already. "I can see that she was a wonderful person and a great boss. But someone killed her, Lucy. There has to be something we're missing. Someone who didn't love her as you do. Someone who wasn't happy with her for some reason. This is where I need your help."

The younger woman dropped her gaze, stared at her hands. Her fingers were clasped together in her lap. The pastel pink uniform of slacks and a double-breasted tunic

with its contrasting while collar was clean and freshly starched. Her white rubber soled shoes were polished to a shine. "Renata added *his* house to my schedule."

Laney frowned at the sudden topic change. "Whose house?"

Lucy lifted her gaze to meet Laney's. "The old recluse." "Please don't say anything. We're not supposed to talk about our clients this way."

"You don't need to worry, Lucy. This conversation is strictly between the two of us."

The other woman nodded.

"Are you referring to Mr. Duval?" Laney supposed he was the closest thing to a recluse they had in Shutter Lake. He rarely left his home that was true. Didn't participate in any community activities as far as she knew. She had visited him twice in the two years she had been deputy chief. Once to take his dog back to him. The beagle had chased a raccoon and ended up at Laney's house. The owner's name and address had been on his collar so she'd taken him home. Duval had thanked her repeatedly. The dog was his only companion. The other time had been to deliver an agenda for a town council meeting. McCabe had hoped the agenda would prompt Duval to attend since the items to be discussed were particularly important, but it hadn't.

"Si. Yes." Lucy moistened her lips. "Sylvie cleaned his home personally. He was one of her first clients and she never allowed anyone else to take care of his home unless she had to go out of town. She said he was special to her, but the rest of us just think he's a little strange. He watches so closely. It's creepy."

This news Laney found surprising. Sylvia never had to lift a finger beyond telling her staff what to do. In the beginning, Laney could understand that she'd worked hard

—despite having wealthy parents—in an effort to gain her independence and to launch her business venture. But she no longer needed to do the grunt work. "Was there anyone else Sylvia took care of personally?"

"No one. Well, there was the Bradshaws, but they discontinued Sparkle services a while back."

There was the tiniest hint of accusation in Lucy's tone. As much as she loved her boss and friend, she sensed something was off with the relationship.

All the possibilities tumbled through Laney's head. Was Sylvia having an affair with the older man? Is that where the stacks of cash in her safe came from? Laney had heard that Duval was loaded. Then again, most of the Shutter Lake residents were. Was he providing drugs to her or vise versa? That theory didn't make sense. Duval never traveled. Rarely left the house. But he did receive mail. The drugs could have been delivered via the mail.

The affair was more likely. Maybe he paid Sylvia for more than polishing his silver. Young women sometimes liked having a sugar daddy. But why would Sylvia need one? Her parents were rich. She had a thriving, very successful business.

The tense interview with Vinn Bradshaw came to mind. Maybe Sylvia liked having an older guy and a younger one, too. Laney put the thought aside for the moment. The high school kid wouldn't have had access to the kind of money found in Sylvia's house. And that money came from somewhere. Odds were it was not from a legal source. Otherwise, why hide it? Why not allow it to draw interest? Rates were good right now.

Laney asked, "Are you afraid of Mr. Duval?" This seemed the most logical possibility for Lucy's discomfort about the man.

She shrugged. "I don't know. Maybe a little. I was there

this morning and he hardly said two words. He sat in front of the fireplace and just stared at the flames. He didn't say nothing to me. Not even hello. We've all heard stories about him." She stared at her hands again. "I really should not say such things. I could get in trouble."

"Remember, Lucy, what you say to me is in confidence. I won't share your personal feelings with anyone, not even Renata."

She nodded her understanding. "I shouldn't judge. It's not right."

"What kind of stories have you heard?" This was news to Laney. She'd never heard a single story, good or bad, about Troy Duval.

"They say he murdered his wife and daughter." She dared to look up at Laney but only for a moment. "He lived in Carmel. His wife was some famous actress. His daughter was just a little girl. They were murdered while he was home."

Laney considered the high profile Hollywood murders she'd heard about growing up. Only one fit the bill Lucy was suggesting. "Are you talking about Madelyn Yates?" Yates and her daughter were murdered, her husband had been in his office, the former pool house, so he wasn't actually in the house when the murders occurred. But he hadn't been more than thirty yards away.

Lucy nodded. "Yes. She was thirty-two and her little girl was seven."

Madelyn Yates and her daughter had been shot and killed—execution style—in their Carmel home some thirty years ago. She remembered seeing the still unsolved mystery on one of those true crime documentary type television programs. "I thought the husband was Jason Lavelle."

"Yes," Lucy confirmed. "He changed his name. Sylvie

said so." Her eyes rounded and her hands went to her mouth.

Laney held up a hand. "No worries, remember?"

Even as she said the words, Laney's heart rate picked up. Had there been a murderer in their midst all this time? One who had gotten away with it before?

Damn.

"Sylvie didn't believe he killed his wife and daughter. She told me it was someone who wanted to hurt him. Revenge or something." Lucy shrugged. "Sylvie was smart. She believed this to be true or she would not have said so."

Laney could certainly understand how a high profile past like that would make a person want to hide in their home for the rest of their lives. She wondered if McCabe knew about this? If he had, wouldn't he have brought it up when discussing potential suspects in Sylvia's murder?

Certainly a question she would be asking him.

"Lucy," Laney considered a moment more how best to frame the question, "did Sylvia ever ask you to do anything special—besides cleaning for the clients?"

The young woman stared at Laney for a moment before the implications of the question sank in, then she shook her head adamantly. "No. No way! Sylvie was very protective of all of us. If anyone had made us feel uncomfortable she would have confronted them immediately. She would never allow such a thing."

"What about drugs? Did Sylvia or any of the clients ever offer drugs to you or accept drugs from you?"

The other woman's forehead furrowed with a frown. "No. Never. Sylvie hated drugs. She has—had a strict no drugs policy. We are not allowed to use drugs and she will not take clients who do."

Exactly the answers Laney had expected. "What about

her finances, did Sylvia ever discuss her finances with you?"

"She had money. Plenty. But she never talked about her money. She was very generous, but she did not speak of it."

Now for the more sensitive territory. "Lucy, were you aware of any sort of relationship between Sylvia and Vinn Bradshaw?"

Lucy pondered the question a moment. "I saw her talk to him once at the market when we ran out of window cleaner. We went there together. The boy was with his mother. He came over and said hello."

"What about his mother? Did she speak to Sylvia as well?"

Lucy shook her head. "No. She never speaks to any of us. Sylvie says she is the definition of a snob." She leaned forward and whispered, "A bitch."

Connie Bradshaw wasn't someone with whom Laney had had reason to interact. They'd spoken in passing on the sidewalk or in a shop. Laney hadn't noticed that she was particularly snobbish. But then she wasn't particularly friendly either.

"Did Sylvia and Mrs. Bradshaw have any problems?"

Lucy shrugged. "I only know what she said that one day."

Another thought occurred to Laney. "You said the Bradshaws stopped being Sparkle's clients. Had they been clients very long?"

"Yes, long time clients until a few months ago. When I first came to work for Sylvie the Bradshaws were scheduled weekly. Maybe six months ago they dropped off the schedule."

"Did Sylvia ever mention why they dropped off the schedule?"

Lucy shook her head. "No. She never talked about it.

Other than people who moved away or died, Sparkle never lost a customer before. It was a big shock. She was upset for some time. Sylvie took it personally."

The Bradshaw name had just moved to the top of the persons of interest list as far as Laney was concerned. When this many threads were dangling there was bound to be a loose seam. Give one thread a pull and the whole thing could unravel.

"Thank you, Lucy."

Laney made her way through the rest of the employees, saving Jennifer Fraley until last. At twenty-eight Fraley was the oldest of the crew. Like the others, she was very attractive. Brown hair, green eyes. Unmarried, as were all the others. No children. With six employees, it seemed odd that they all just happened to be single and childless. Or maybe not, they were all young, in their twenties.

"How long have you been with Sparkle?" Laney started out with the questions to which she knew the answers. This way she could get a feel for Fraley's honest answers. McCabe had questioned her yesterday so this was Laney's first time speaking directly to her.

"Five years."

Fraley stated her answer and nothing more. Time to shake things up. "You moved from San Francisco to Shutter Lake around five years ago after a prostitution charge and spending a few months in jail. Did you know someone here? If not, why choose this town?"

"Renata and I went to high school together," Fraley said. "After they cut me loose, I was desperate. I'd heard through the grapevine that she was doing good for herself. I just needed a hand. I wanted to do better."

"Were Renata and Sylvia aware of your previous profession?"

Fraley's face tightened the slightest bit. "Yeah. I was up

front with Renata when I called her and she told Sylvie about my past. Sylvie wanted to help me. She was like that, you know."

Laney nodded. "I'd like you to be up front with me, too, Jennifer. How long were you in the life?"

She crossed her arms over her pink tunic and jutted out her chin. "I dropped out of high school at sixteen after my father kicked me out. Friends took me in for a while, but before long I had no place to go, nothing to eat and no skill to change those two facts. So I sold my body to survive. I'm sure all of this is in a file somewhere at City Hall."

It was now. They'd run each of the employees' names and Fraley's record popped up. "But you were determined to change that after your arrest."

"I didn't want to go back. I wanted a real life. Sylvie gave me that chance."

In the past twenty-four hours Laney had heard endless testimonials about what an awesome person Sylvia Cole was. It wasn't that she doubted any of the heartfelt accolades but when something or someone sounded too good to be true, they generally were. There were certain facts that could not be denied. First, Sylvia opened the door to her killer, which meant she most likely knew him. Second, she was in a nightshirt. Even more reason to believe she knew her killer well. Murder was always precipitated by a motive of some sort, but when the murderer is a familiar, then the motive is particularly strong. Her killer not only had a compelling reason to despise Sylvia enough to want her dead—that reason was powerful enough to do it up close, shoving any affection aside. He wanted her to look him in the eye as she struggled to breathe. He wanted her to know he was the one killing her.

Was Vinn Bradshaw not ready to end his relationship

with Sylvia? Did he have the courage and strength to commit such an up close and intimate murder?

Had Sylvia learned some secret about Troy Duval? Maybe that he really had murdered his wife and daughter?

Was all that cash in Sylvia's closet because she was running more than a cleaning service? Maybe carrying out a little blackmail?

"Jennifer," the other woman's eyes met Laney's, "was Sylvia doing anything illegal?"

"What?" She made an are-you-insane face. "No way!"

"She never asked any of you to do anything illegal for her?"

Fury darkened Fraley's face now. "Are you suggesting that just because all of us are young and pretty that we were servicing our clients in other ways?"

"No." Laney shook her head. "I'm not suggesting anything. I'm *asking* if you were."

"Son of a…" She took a deep breath. "We're all clean. Spotless! Sylvie made us all take drug tests every month. Always when we least expected it. We were warned on a regular basis that if a client ever reported something missing or damaged that we didn't report first, we were gone. If we got personally involved with a client, we were gone. No debating, no questions. Gone. Done. Fired. Reputation was everything to her."

"Is that what happened to Josie Rodriquez? Did she break one of those rules?"

Based on how Sylvia treated her employees, there had to be a strong reason Rodriquez was gone.

Fraley shrugged. "I don't know what happened with her. She was a hard worker. Always on time. Never got into trouble. She just didn't come back one day. Sylvie was surprised and worried. I know she made a lot of calls trying to find her, but never did as far as I know."

"This was two, two and a half months ago?"

"Yeah. Sylvie was helping Josie with her papers." Fraley gave Laney a look. "You know, her citizenship papers. Josie seemed really excited. Then she was just gone."

"No one's heard from her since the last day she showed up for work?"

"Not a word."

"You're certain she and Sylvia never had any issues?"

A scenario was forming fast for Laney. Rodriquez had been young, only seventeen, according to her file. What if she was the one who was involved with Vinn Bradshaw? But then why would Vinn wait until a few days ago to confront Sylvia for sending her away? Laney would add that to the follow up questions she had for Vinn—assuming the lawyer allowed any more questions.

Laney studied the woman seated across the desk from her. As forthcoming as all Sylvia's employees had been, it still felt as if they were all leaving something out. She clasped her hands on the desk in front of her. "We really need answers here, Jennifer. I know all of you believe Sylvia was an amazing person—a godsend in many ways—but she must have had at least one secret. Something someone was willing to kill for."

Fraley stared at Laney for a long moment before she responded. "Everyone has secrets, Deputy Holt. I'll bet you even have a few."

Laney smiled. "I have one or two, yes."

"This town is a lot like you, then. When people look at it, they see a beautiful place. A calm and quiet place. But there are secrets. Way more than anyone would ever imagine. You just have to look closely to see them."

Laney's heart was pounding by the time Fraley fell

silent once more. "Are any of those secrets the reason Sylvia was murdered?"

Fraley shrugged. "You tell me, you're the cop."

The interview went downhill from there. The women weren't allowed to discuss their clients. Each employee signed a contract that explicitly prohibited the disclosure of details related to clients or the discussing of anything they learned from a client or at a client's home. The only exception to that rule was with the conveying of that information to Sylvia or to Renata. Lucy was the only one to even skirt close to breaking that rule. And all insisted there were no drugs and no other illegal activities.

After thanking Renata for her cooperation, Laney headed back to City Hall. She had some background to dig up on Troy Duval before going to interview him. She also intended to see if she could locate Josie Rodriguez. Since she was no longer employed by Sparkle, maybe she would be willing to talk.

Then there was the Bradshaw family. Laney needed to know why the Bradshaws had dropped Sparkle as their cleaning service.

Had one of the girls broken a golden rule with the teenage son?

At the end of the day, Laney intended to have a sit down with McCabe. She had a feeling there was a lot more to his relationship with Vernon Bradshaw than anyone knew. Whether it was relevant or not, Laney needed it off her list of loose ends.

Plus, McCabe should know at least some of the secrets folks in Shutter Lake were keeping. If he didn't, maybe his father would—except his father was in the nursing home with dementia.

It seemed each step forward was immediately followed

by two steps back. Maybe Laney was rusty. She hadn't played the role of homicide detective in over two years.

Outside the sun was shining, bringing the temperature to that lovely sixty degrees the meteorologist had forecast on last night's news. Laney took her time walking back to City Hall. Jennifer Fraley was right about everyone seeing what they wanted to see when they looked at Shutter Lake. Beauty, tranquility, happiness.

Except the residents of this town were mere humans, just like Laney, just like Fraley. All humans had weaknesses, most had secrets.

Sylvia Cole had secrets just like everyone else. It was looking more and more like one or more of her secrets had gotten her killed.

All Laney had to do was figure out which secret it was and she would find the killer.

As horrible as the murder was, as shaken as the entire community was…how were they going to react when they discovered that the killer was one of them?

CHAPTER EIGHT

Troy leaned back in his seat, set the rocker in motion with his feet. He loved sitting on his front porch this time of day. His gardens and small vineyard were done for the season. He was always sad when the last of the vegetables and grapes had been harvested. The work occupied his hands and his mind.

He clasped his hands in his lap. Shivered a bit no matter that he'd pulled on a fleece-lined jacket over his flannel shirt. But it wasn't the temperature that chilled his bones. An ache pierced him so thoroughly he lost his breath.

Sylvia was dead.

He closed his eyes and fought back the burn of tears. Sweet, sweet Sylvia.

She was dead and it was his fault. He was certain. His eyes opened and he dragged in a rattling breath.

Perhaps a cup of tea would warm him. He braced both hands on the wooden arms of the rocking chair and levered himself up. His body was thin and frail now and growing weaker all the time. For years he had suffered little or no symptoms of the Multiple Sclerosis now ravaging his body. He'd received the diagnosis ten years ago at age sixty. Late-onset, they called it. The drugs had warded off the worst issues for all that time, he supposed. But now, the weakness, tremors and myriad other symptoms were his constant companion. His doctor had already suggested that he consider live-in care for the near future. He hadn't decided if he preferred the coming helplessness or a bullet to the brain.

Sylvia had helped him for the past few years. She saw to it that his supplies were ordered and delivered from the supermarket and she personally picked up his prescriptions. Ms. Fernandez had assured him that the new woman coming to his home would take care of all his needs, but he wasn't certain about this other woman yet.

She stared at him. Crept around like a frightened child. She was not Sylvia.

Sylvia was gone.

His heart squeezed as he shuffled into the house. The new woman's housekeeping skills were more than adequate but she had no personality. She brought no happiness to his home. He had looked forward to Sylvia's weekly visits. He wouldn't have cared if she hadn't bothered with cleaning at all. Basking in her presence had been enough.

By the time he made it to the kitchen he was panting. Hand trembling, he settled the kettle onto the stove eye and lit the flame beneath it with a twist of the knob. Slowly, he gathered a mug and the box of Earl Grey that was his favorite. Another struggle was required to reach the refrigerator and get the cream, then the sugar. Finally, he had everything he needed. The water had already started to boil, prompting that high-pitched whistle.

Once he'd poured the water, he made his way to the living room and sat in his favorite chair in front of the fireplace. He fumbled for the remote, turned on the gas logs. A few minutes were required to catch his breath, by then the tea was the perfect temperature for drinking.

He should never have advised Sylvia and she would be alive today.

Anguish raged through his soul. He had wanted to help her. He hadn't wanted her to end up as miserable as his precious Madelyn had been. She had allowed those Hollywood elitists to keep knocking her down. More than once, before they met, she had been taken advantage of by the egotistical men who ran that town in those days. Bastards. They had beaten her down until she was nothing but a shell of the beauty she had once been.

But then she and Troy had met. He helped her to rise above her painful past. He infused her with confidence and financed her work. When their angel, Madison, was born, their lives had been complete. Troy had been certain their lives were perfect. Except his precious wife was tricked into becoming involved with another of those bastards who ruled the industry with an iron fist. Too embarrassed to come to Troy for help, she had tried to extricate herself from the situation on her own. The bastard had hurt her and Troy had reacted. The man had no idea that Troy had once been a military assassin for the country of his birth. He studied this evil man, learned what he loved most—his secret male lover—and ended the lover's life. But the man repaid him in spades. He took Madelyn and Madison from Troy. He'd even managed to lay the groundwork to cast enough suspicion to have the police believing Troy was the one who killed them.

Coming here to this quiet place far away from the sea —away from the horror of his past—had given Troy a place to lock himself away. He'd sentenced himself to live in agony. God knew he had wanted to kill himself at least once everyday the past thirty years, but he had refused to let himself off so easily. Living with what he had done was his punishment. Then Sylvia came into his life.

She had given him something to live for again.

In return, he had killed her as surely as he had his beloved family.

He remembered vividly the day he put the idea in her head. A terrible, terrible mistake.

Five years ago...

"You are a beautiful young woman, Sylvia. You should be sure to take care of yourself. Never allow anyone to rule you."

She laughed. Her laughter was like tinkling bells, soft and melodic. "Mr. Duval, I have never allowed anyone to rule me. Just ask my father."

"Knowledge is power, young lady. Always remember that," he advised. "Make it a point to know every single thing you can about those around you and you will always be in charge."

She sat down on the ottoman directly in front of his chair, her blue eyes glittering. "What kinds of things, Mr. Duval?"

"All kinds." He smiled. "Learn a person's deepest, darkest secrets and you will own them."

She laughed again. "I don't know about that. There are a lot of brilliant, powerful people in this town. My father knows all of them. They're all friends." She shrugged her slender shoulders. "My company cleans their homes."

"You are in their homes," he reminded her with a wink. "Their deepest, darkest secrets are right there. Find them, memorize them and then use them if the necessity arises. That way, no one will ever own you. You will always have the upper hand. Knowledge is the ultimate power, my dear."

She searched his eyes. "Why are you telling me this now, Mr.

Duval? I've been cleaning your house for three years. You were one of my first customers."

"I had to wait until the time was right. Until you were mature enough to understand the power you possess."

She made a face. "What power?"

"You are beautiful, Sylvia. Beautiful, smart and ambitious. Never allow anyone to take that from you. Arm yourself with the proper ammunition. You will thank me one day."

She had thanked him. Before she left for the day after her final weekly visit, she hugged him and whispered, "Thank you, Mr. Duval. You were right. Knowledge is power."

Now she was dead.

CHAPTER NINE

Troy Duval's home sat at the end of the road that ran parallel to Laney's. A jaunt through the woods across the road from her house would bring her into his backyard, which is how his beagle ended up at her house. His home, a log cabin that was more of a mansion than a cabin, bumped against the woods with the larger portion of his property spreading out in front of his house.

She turned into the driveway, rolled up to the keypad and entered the temporary code Duval had given her. The massive iron gates opened, allowing her to roll forward. The driveway was a long one, winding down and through the vineyard. Closer to the house what appeared to be a vegetable garden was on the right while a parking area waited on the left. The fifteen-year-old SUV registered to Duval was apparently in the garage.

Laney climbed out of her car and walked to the front porch. The wind was up a little but the sun was warm. She climbed the steps, still mulling over the best starting place for the interview. She knocked on the door and listened. No sound inside. She knocked again.

"Let yourself in."

The words were muffled but loud enough to hear. She opened the door and leaned in. "Mr. Duval?"

"In the great room by the fire."

Laney closed the door behind her and followed the direction of his voice. The entry hall opened into an enormous great room. As he'd said, he sat in a chair in front of the fire. The stone fireplace was wide and soared to the roofline of the cathedral style ceiling.

"Please join me, Deputy Holt." He gestured to the other chair facing the fireplace. "I took the liberty of preparing tea, if you're interested."

A ceramic pot, sugar bowl and tiny creamer pitcher, along with two mugs waited on the tray he'd placed on the table between the two chairs.

"Tea would be nice."

She sat down in the large chair. Everything about the home was oversized. But then, Duval was a tall man. Though he was thin and looked frail now, she'd looked up photos of him as a younger man. He had been quite tall, broad shouldered and well muscled. This was a mere shell of the man he once was. She suspected a serious medical condition but couldn't be sure.

"I have Earl Grey and Vanilla Chai."

Quite a contrast in flavors. "I'll take the Chai. Thank you."

He placed a bag in one of the mugs and poured the steaming water. "This was Sylvia's favorite tea. I kept it for her. Sugar or cream?"

"Both please." When he'd passed her the mug she thanked him and he took his seat. The effort he'd expended visibly taking the wind out of his sails.

"I cannot tell you how devastated I am by Sylvia's

death." He exhaled a breath, laden with the same heavy sadness Laney saw in his eyes. "She was a dear friend."

"I didn't know her personally," Laney felt compelled to tell him. "But everyone I've spoken to adored her." The Bradshaws could go either way, but Vinn certainly appeared to have strong feelings about Sylvia. Maybe his mother did as well.

"She was a bright light in this dark world." Duval sipped his tea.

Laney did the same, allowing the hot tea to warm her. It was a fairly warm day but inside she felt cold. Investigating murder had a way of putting a chill in her bones. "I'll have to get this brand of tea," she noted before taking another sip. "It's really quite good."

"It's available at the local market." He placed his mug on the tray. "But you didn't come here to discuss the nuances of good tea."

"I did not." Laney set her mug aside as well. "Based on the cause of death, we have reason to believe Sylvia was murdered by someone she knew. Probably someone she knew well. Because of that evidence, it's important that we speak to everyone close to her."

"I rarely leave the house." He chuckled but there was no humor in the sound. "I have MS, Deputy Holt. I hardly have the strength to walk from room to room. I couldn't have killed Sylvia or anyone else, even if I felt so inclined."

The Multiple Sclerosis certainly explained his declining condition. "I'm sorry to hear that, Mr. Duval. You understand how important it is that we turn over every rock. Particularly if there is any history—suggested or otherwise —of violence."

"Ah." He nodded knowingly. "You uncovered my big secret. Exhumed the skeletons in my past."

Laney couldn't help feeling a little guilty bringing up the man's past. No one hated reliving the past anymore than she did. But this sore spot was a necessary wound to reopen. Duval was far too intelligent to be fooled by any other excuse.

"More reporters have flocked to Shutter Lake," she admitted. "How long do you suppose it will be before one of them figures out who you are? If the question arises, the chief and I need to be able to head off any trouble for you that might be roused. The more knowledgeable we sound, the less likely anyone is to go off digging for answers."

He nodded. "I see your point. So you want my story. Very well. I'll tell you all there is to know—all I know."

"I appreciate your cooperation, sir. No one wants to find the person responsible for this senseless death more than I do."

His pale, silvery eyes held Laney's gaze a long moment. "I believe you do, Deputy. So, where would you like me to start?"

"Why do you believe your wife and daughter were murdered?"

He sighed. "Revenge. There was a man—if you read the case file you'll know the one I mean—who held a position of power at the studio where Madelyn was working to rebuild her career. This man liked having what he wanted and he wanted my wife. When she attempted to extricate herself from the situation, he found a reason to cancel her contract for the upcoming series that would have put her back on the map, so to speak. She was devastated."

The rest was easy to guess. "You felt compelled to settle the issue."

"I did."

"Will it do me any good to ask how you settled it?"

"No." His gaze met hers. "Trust me when I say I have paid many times for that poor decision. This powerful man had my wife and daughter killed right under my nose while I was working in my home office." He laughed that dry sound again. "I was writing a novel about murder and treachery. Ironic, isn't it?" He stared into the flames.

"Could this man or someone close to him still be watching you? Perhaps he decided to take something else from you. Or maybe there is someone you haven't mentioned who feels he or she was once slighted by you?"

He shook his head. "The man who had my wife and child murdered died shortly after their deaths. He drowned in his own hot tub. The medical examiner ruled his death an accident. One should never over indulge in mind altering substances and then climb into the water. Not very smart."

Laney wasn't surprised to hear that ending. What did surprise her was that he almost admitted to murdering the man.

"As for your second question, there is no one else, believe me."

To her surprise, she did. "Do you have any thoughts on who might have wanted to hurt Sylvia?"

He continued to stare at the flames, his head moving from side to side. "If I did, I would certainly tell you. I cannot imagine anyone wanting to hurt her. She was a good person. A caring person."

"I've been hearing that all morning." His eyes met hers then. "But someone didn't feel that way. Someone killed her."

"Someone who knew her, you said," he responded.

"We believe so."

"Start with the clients of her business. Beyond her family, I suspect they knew her better than anyone and vise versa."

"Do you have reason to believe one of her clients wanted to hurt her?"

"No." His gaze wandered back to the flames when he said this.

"Tell me about the last time you saw, Sylvia."

"She was here on Wednesdays. That was her day with me."

Interesting. "The day she was murdered."

He flinched. "Yes, I suppose so."

"Did she act any different? Maybe she had something on her mind? Seemed distracted?"

"No." He turned to face Laney. "Sylvia was her usual happy self. If she had a problem in the world, she showed no indication."

"Did she mention any plans she had for that night? Maybe she was going to dinner or having someone over?"

"If she had plans, she said nothing about them."

"Do you know if she was involved romantically with anyone?"

"No one she ever spoke about."

"What time did she leave your home, Mr. Duval?"

"Around three. She generally arrived at eight." He smiled sadly. "She always brought me a bagel or a muffin from The Grind. She worked all morning, then we played catch up at lunch. She would tell me what was going on in her world and then she'd work a couple more hours and leave. It was the highlight of my week. I am lost without her."

Laney couldn't help feeling sorry for him. How sad it must be to reach his age and to be all alone. *Isn't that exactly where you're headed, Laney?* She cleared her head of the static. "Did she tell you anything new about what was going on in her world this past Wednesday?"

"She was very excited about a vacation. She hasn't

taken one since the last time she went with her parents as a teenager. She had planned an extended trip to Venezuela."

Laney couldn't recall the last time she'd taken a vacation. "Any particular reason she chose Venezuela?"

"Not that she mentioned."

Laney removed a business card from her jacket pocket and placed it on the tray next to the teapot. "I hope you'll call me if you think of anything else that might be useful to our investigation."

"I will. Yes."

Laney stood. Duval reached to push up from his chair and she held her hands up. "Please, I can see myself out."

He nodded. "Good luck with the investigation, Deputy."

Before she turned away, she asked, "How is your beagle? Archie?" She hadn't seen him outside and he didn't appear to be in the house.

Duval sighed. "I'm afraid he passed just a few months ago. Sylvia helped me bury him near his favorite tree. It was another sad day."

"I'm sorry to hear that."

Laney thanked him again and left his home. The gate opened as she approached and she drove on through. She appreciated that Duval seemed happy to be so open with her. The only part of the interview that nudged her instincts was his inability to maintain eye contact after certain questions.

What else besides an old murder was the man hiding?

She would be coming back to that question. For now, she drove over to Sierra College. Based on Shonda Reed's class schedule she would be leaving her first class of the day at three. She had a half hour break before the next one. Laney intended to be waiting outside the lecture hall. She had questions for Shonda but she didn't want to talk to her where Nolan Ikard might hear about it.

When the doors of the lecture hall opened and students started to file out, Laney pushed off the wall where she'd been leaning and watched for Shonda. While she'd waited she had checked in with the lab. McCabe had gotten the prints from the table to the lab but they hadn't been processed just yet. The sheets were definitely loaded with semen but finding a match would take time and then only if the person who left the body fluid behind was in the database. No useable prints from the victim's throat or anywhere else on her body. No skin under her nails. That was about the extent of the relevant evidence they had so far. Nothing that would help unless they found a match and even then the killer wasn't necessarily the man with whom Sylvia had sex. The semen could have been from the night before for that matter.

Shonda Reed, petite, strawberry blond hair, big brown eyes, bounced from the lecture hall. She was deep in discussion with another woman and didn't notice Laney until she called her name.

Shonda turned, spotted Laney and froze. Her friend said something and she blinked, responded and then her friend moved on.

Laney walked across the carpeted corridor toward the younger woman who looked exactly like a trapped animal with no place to run. "Hey, Shonda. I was hoping we could talk for a bit."

"Sure. I have a few minutes before my next class."

"We can walk that way," Laney offered. No need to cause her to be late.

Shonda nodded, the movement jerky. "Yeah, okay."

They exited the building and the sun was still bright though it was dropping toward the treetops.

"Are you aware of your boss's relationship with Sylvia Cole?"

She glanced at Laney, her eyes wide. "Relationship? What do you mean?"

"They had been friends for a really long time." That part was true. "A few people I've interviewed suggested they were more than friends."

Shonda shrugged. "I don't know about that. I mean, they flirted like crazy with each other. But I can't say they were anything other than friends. Nolan flirts a lot with a lot of women."

"Hmm. You seemed surprised when he told me they were only friends."

She stared straight ahead. "I did? I don't know why I would have. I wasn't really paying that much attention to your conversation."

Laney stopped. Shonda did the same, almost stumbling. "I think you're lying to me, Shonda. And that bothers me. You see, I have a job to do and I can't do it if people lie to me."

Shonda winced. Quickly wiped the surprise off her face and went for nonchalant. "I'm not sure what your feelings and conclusions have to do with me."

"I think you know that Nolan and Sylvia were intimately involved and you were surprised he didn't tell me the truth. People who don't have anything to hide usually tell the truth, don't they?"

The younger woman blinked. "Well, yes, I guess so."

"Then why do you suppose he lied?"

"He's..." She swallowed, licked her lips.

"Better yet," Laney pushed, "why are you lying?"

"I suppose he's scared that he'll be blamed for hurting

Sylvia. You can't always trust the cops. I mean, this is a kind of scary moment. You're like freaking me out."

Shonda had no criminal record. Ikard didn't either, for that matter. "Why would I be freaking out an innocent person? Do you or Nolan have reason to distrust me or anyone else in the Shutter Lake Police Department?"

She shook her head. "No. It's just that with everything you see on the news, you never know."

That part was, sadly, true. "We aren't on the news, Shonda. We're here and I'm trying to find a killer. If you want to help me do that then you shouldn't be afraid to tell me the truth, should you?"

"I guess not." Her fingers tightened around the strap of the backpack hanging off one shoulder.

"Were Nolan and Sylvia more than friends?"

She nodded. "I think they were like *buddies*, you know? Shared a physical relationship that had nothing to do with love or complicated relationship stuff. A no strings attached kind of thing."

"How long do you believe they've had this more intimate relationship?"

A shrug lifted her slender shoulders. "I've worked at The Grind for a year and they were, you know, intimate already when I joined the team."

"Did you ever hear them argue? Or maybe Sylvia mentioned someone who was giving her trouble? Another guy, possibly?"

For about five seconds the younger girl chewed her bottom lip, then she said, "There's this one high school kid, Vinn Bradshaw. He came into The Grind once when Sylvia was there. He seemed really upset that she was flirting with Nolan. But I can't be sure. He might have been upset about something else. Anyway, he and Sylvia went outside. I couldn't hear what they were saying, but it looked like they were arguing."

"What did Nolan do? Did he seem upset about what was happening?"

"He just said the kid needed to get a life and stop fantasizing about things he couldn't have."

"But Nolan didn't give you any indication that he was angry or upset?"

"No way. He's the king of cool. Very little ever upsets him. Besides, like I said, I don't think whatever he and Sylvia had was like a real relationship. It was just a way to get off, you know."

Laney understood perfectly. "When was the last time Sylvia dropped by the shop?"

"Wednesday morning. She came in about seven-thirty, got bagels for her and Mr. Duval. She did that every Wednesday. She was always doing nice stuff for people."

Shonda had just confirmed that aspect of Duval's story, not that Laney doubted him. She hadn't gotten the impression that he was lying. Maybe not being totally forthcoming about how much he cared about Sylvia and who might have had reason to hurt her, but he hadn't murdered her. Laney doubted he knew who had or that person might be dead already. Since no other bodies had popped up in Shutter Lake, she felt reasonably confident he was in the clear on that score.

That said, she had a feeling that Troy Duval, formerly Jason Lavelle, knew the kind of people who could slip in and commit murder and make it look like an accident without ever leaving a trace of evidence.

"Did Sylvia seem okay that morning?" Laney asked. "She wasn't upset or behaving differently than usual?"

Shonda thought about the question for a bit before

answering. "She seemed excited. She mentioned a vacation. Maybe that's why."

Laney wondered why no one at Sparkle had mentioned that Sylvia was planning a vacation. Surely Renata Fernandez would know her boss's plans.

"Was Nolan going with her?"

Shonda frowned. "No. He said he wouldn't go anywhere that required a passport. Too many young people—especially pretty ones like Sylvia—disappearing."

"Like being kidnapped? Human trafficking?"

Shonda nodded. "Yeah. Venezuela is like in the top five of the worst countries for human trafficking. I told Sylvia she was crazy to go there alone."

"Did she say why she wanted to go there?"

"She just said, she wanted to go someplace new."

"Thank you, Shonda. You've been a great help." Laney gave her a card. "Please call me if you think of anything else."

She stared at the card then at Laney. "You're not going to tell Nolan what I said, are you?"

"Nope. This conversation is just between the two of us." And the chief, but she didn't bother tacking on that part.

By the time Laney got back to the office it was just after four. She went straight to her office and did some research that had been needling her all afternoon and then she walked across the hall to McCabe's office and knocked. Both their offices had windows but the blinds on the chief's were closed. She hoped he didn't have anyone in there.

"Come on in!"

Laney opened the door and walked in. "I was worried you had a visitor."

He shook his head. "Just needed some time to think. I hope you've had better luck today than me." He leaned back in his chair. "Close the door and have a seat."

Laney pushed the door closed and dropped into the chair in front of his desk. "Tell me about yours and I'll tell you about mine."

One corner of his mouth lifted in a hint of a smile but it didn't last long. "I tried to talk to Vernon and he blew me off." McCabe shook his head. "He warned me to stay away from his son. It's the damnedest thing. I have known this guy and his family my whole life. I don't know what's up, but it can't be good. I also talked to the folks at the lab."

"Yeah, I called them, too. Nothing useful yet."

He grunted a sound of frustration. "I also called the coroner's office. They reminded me that autopsies take time. Everything takes time. And I want answers now." He blew out a big breath of frustration. "On top of that, we can officially rule out robbery."

Now this was news. "How so?"

"A jogger found her credit cards and sixty bucks in cash in the ditch about two miles from her house. The woman and her mutt showed up with the stuff in one of those doggie poop bags."

Laney laughed, couldn't help herself. "Since she didn't own any fine jewelry pieces that anyone is aware of, you're right, robbery is off the table." Not that she ever really thought that was the motive.

"So what kind of progress did you make?"

"I interviewed Troy Duval. I think we can slide his name to the bottom of our list. There may be things he knows that he didn't share, but I believe he will in *time*." Laney flashed a fake smile. "In my opinion, particularly considering he has MS and is very frail, we can safely put him in the *didn't do it* category."

McCabe made a couple of notes on his ever-handy yellow pad.

"I talked to Nolan Ikard and Shonda Reed. Ikard didn't admit as much, but Reed confirmed that he and our victim had a more intimate relationship without all the strings. She also mentioned that Vinn Bradshaw showed up at the coffee shop. He and Sylvia had a tense conversation outside. I think we have to assume that something was happening between Sylvia and Vinn or maybe just that he wanted something to happen. Whether the Bradshaws want us nosing around or not, we can't ignore all the facts."

"You're right. Anything else?"

Laney considered the other and decided it was definitely relevant. "Although her employees didn't mention anything about it, Sylvia was apparently planning a vacation to Venezuela. Alone."

McCabe shrugged. "Okay."

"Venezuela, as I just heard and then verified, is like one of the top five cities in the world for human trafficking issues."

"Sylvia was pretty fearless."

Laney nodded. "From all accounts totally fearless. Here's the kicker. That employee of hers that just up and left, Josie Rodriquez."

McCabe went still as if the adrenaline suddenly pumping in Laney's veins had started firing in his as well. "Yeah."

"I did some research on her. She didn't just leave. Her folks over in Grass Valley have her listed as missing. Young, beautiful, missing for going on three months now."

"You're thinking she was a victim of human trafficking

and Sylvia was somehow trying to find her—hence the vacation to Venezuela."

"It's a theory I want to follow up on. And just maybe our super intelligent boy Vinn was actually romantically involved with young Josie and had been pushing Sylvia to look into it. Maybe that's what all the tension was about."

"You're good, Holt." McCabe's smile was real this time. "I'm damn glad you're here."

CHAPTER TEN

Laney pulled to the curb on Mill Street in front of the house where Dana Perkins resided. The principal lived a good deal more frugally than many of the other residents. Her small white bungalow was only a block from the school. No matter that the house was small, it was charming. Houses had personalities and this one suited Dana. Laney drove past the school every morning on her way to work. Dana walked to school, weather permitting, and never failed to wave.

Dana had never been married, no children. No criminal record, of course. She was well thought of in the community. She attended fitness classes at the wellness center and was always the first to volunteer for community fundraisers. She made Laney tired just thinking about the number of pies her fingers were in. And the woman still had time to be a good friend and show up at the occasional girls' night.

Since her car was parked next to the house and the kitchen light glowed through the window, Dana was likely home. Laney emerged from her car and headed up the sidewalk. Dusk was closing in. Most folks were probably settling in for dinner. Laney had stayed at the office doing more research on human trafficking before calling it a day. Though she couldn't see how Sylvia's decision to go looking for the missing woman in another country would have caused her murder here, it was a lead Laney refused to ignore.

She climbed the steps and rang the doorbell. Something that sounded like "coming" echoed on the other side of the door, a few seconds later it opened. The scent of searing veggies and exotic oils wafted out, reminding Laney that she should eat.

"Laney." Dana smiled but then the expression faded. "Has something else happened?"

Her reaction was the same fear simmering in the whole community. All these years not a single violent crime, much less a murder, and now everyone was terrified that another murder was imminent.

"No. Thankfully nothing else has happened. I just have a few questions for you, if you have a moment."

"Of course! Come in." She opened the door wider. "Let me make sure I turned off the stove." She closed the door.

"I don't want to keep you from your dinner." It sure smelled good. Laney's mouth watered and that rarely happened anymore. She'd lost the desire for food at the same time her life fell apart. No matter that she'd pulled herself back together fairly well, some things hadn't revived. Her appetite was one of them. At least until about five seconds ago.

"It's mostly done. I just have to stir the rice." Her mouth rounded with a quickly indrawn breath. "Why don't you have dinner with me? I always prepare too much and God knows the leftovers always go to waste."

"I'm sure you've had a long day. You don't need to worry about feeding me."

"Come," Dana countered, "have a seat at the island. I insist." She grinned. "You can ask me anything you like as long as you eat."

Laney decided not to argue. She was tired and hungry and whatever was on that stove smelled divine. She settled onto a stool. The main living area of the house was one long, open room. Beyond the kitchen was a hallway that led to the private rooms. Dana's style was modern and relaxed. No clutter. No fuss. Nice. But what Laney found the most amazing was on the stove. A wok was filled with colorful veggies and sizzled with the most incredible smell. Next to the wok a saucepan brimmed with fluffy white rice.

"I make this every week," Dana was saying. "I love Asian food but they add so much salt when you buy it at the grocery store or even at restaurants. I prepare it myself so I can control what I put in."

"Very smart." Laney's shoulders relaxed for the first time today. "I really should learn to cook. I mean, I make a mean scrambled egg, but that's about the extent of my culinary skills."

Dana laughed, the sound was pleasant. She looked very much at home in front of that stove. The stovetop was actually a part of the island, making conversation easy even with her deep into meal prep.

"You'll notice I love bright colors."

This was true. There were strips of red and yellow bell peppers. Something green that Laney decided was zucchini. Dana spread a bed of rice on a plate, then spooned veggies, chicken and sauce atop it. She placed it in front of Laney.

"It looks and smells fantastic."

"What would you like to drink?" Dana prepared

another plate as she talked. "I have wine and water and I think I might have a couple of sodas."

"Water would be great." Wine would have been nice, too, but Laney was on the clock.

Once the drinks were prepared and Dana was settled on the stool next to Laney's, they ate for a while before she broached her first question.

"You've been the principal at Shutter Lake School for a good many years now."

"Seven," Dana said, then sipped her wine.

"So you've known Vinn Bradshaw and his family for a while."

"I have."

Laney forked a pepper and took a bite. Let her friend think about the direction of the question for a moment. When she'd swallowed she asked, "have there ever been any problems with him? Not necessarily anything big, just little issues that you may have noticed."

Another sip of wine and she turned to Laney. "Vinn is a very good boy. Quiet. Kind. Never in any sort of trouble. He's very much a momma's boy, so to speak. His father is quite demanding and I think perhaps that's the reason he is more drawn to his mother. Honestly, I can't say that I've ever noted any issues whatsoever with Vinn."

"What about his parents? You've been around them at school functions. Basketball games. Anything you've noticed that seemed off or volatile?"

"His parents appear quite close." She picked at her rice. "Happy as far as I can tell. Vinn has never complained about life at home. Generally if there are issues at home we hear about them at school or, at least, see the repercussions."

Laney thought of what Duval and Fraley said about secrets. "You've never felt as if Vinn was hiding anything or covering up any secrets? His work has never suffered? No attitude issues?"

Dana paused, her wine midway to her mouth. "You know, there was a short period about three months ago when he seemed out of sorts. Nothing shocking, but noticeable. He maintains a perfect four point oh, but his grades did slip a little there for a week or two. Then he pulled everything back where it should be. But yes," she met Laney's gaze, "something must have happened. He never spoke about it, but there's no other explanation."

They ate for a while longer without speaking.

Dana asked, "Are you thinking Vinn knows something about what happened to Sylvia?"

Laney would like to say no, but that would be a lie. "We have reason to believe that he was aware of some issue going on with Sylvia prior to her murder. I'm not saying he was involved, but he knows something and he's not sharing."

"He wasn't forthcoming in your interview?"

Laney shook her head. "The biggest thing we learned from the interview is that he's very angry with his father. Was there something going on with his father when you noticed the slip in his grades?"

Dana put her fork down and sighed. "I wish I could tell you but he never talked to anyone about whatever was bothering him. Vinn is very private."

"Does he have any particularly close friends he might confide in?"

"Vinn is well liked. I would absolutely say that anyone in his class would be considered a friend, but I think he's closest to Kristina Sharapova. She's a Russian exchange student living with the Windermeres."

"Is she his girlfriend?" If so that could potentially downplay the idea that he was obsessed with Sylvia.

"No, I don't think so. I think they're just friends. They spend a good deal of time together. I always see them in the lunchroom seated at the same table. Any time they're both in the same place, they stay close."

Laney added the Sharapova girl to her list of people to interview. "Is there anyone else you think Vinn might talk to?"

"I suppose he might complain about his home life to any one of his classmates if the subject came up. I mean, it's possible. Teenagers at times bemoan their lot in life to one another the same as we adults do."

An idea occurred to Laney but she wasn't sure the principal would be willing to go along with the plan. She would never know if she didn't ask. "Dana, you also serve as the school psychologist."

"That's right. Our school is just too small to consider hiring another staff member and it's difficult to find someone with those sorts of credentials who's willing to accept a part time position and, possibly, to relocate."

"As a psychologist you would want to take steps to reassure your students and perhaps to help them work through their feelings related to the murder. In a small town like this a violent act is far closer to home, so to speak. Most of the kids probably knew Sylvia, at least had met her."

Dana hesitated a moment before responding. "We've had an assembly with the older students to discuss what happened, if that's what you mean."

"It is, yes. Have you considered having the older students, maybe the juniors and seniors write about how this tragedy affected them or someone they know?"

"Ah, I see where you're going with this. If one appears to know something useful to the investigation, then I pass it along to you."

"I know it's a lot to ask," Laney admitted, "but if it helps us find Sylvia's murderer…"

"I don't like using my students."

Laney feared she would find the suggestion a little too scheming. "But if it helps the students protect themselves and the community, what's the harm? There could be others who saw something or know something—as we suspect Vinn does—who are afraid to tell anyone."

The thought gave Dana pause. Laney mentally crossed her fingers.

"Okay." Dana nodded. "Since it's Friday, I'll take the weekend to figure out the best way to approach the request and I'll let you know on Monday."

"It can't hurt," Laney urged. "And there's a chance it could help us find a killer."

As Laney drove back through town, heading home, she surveyed the rows of lovely little shops in full fall and Halloween regalia. Folks on the sidewalks moved toward restaurants, talking and laughing. She made the turn, driving past City Hall. She'd almost passed it when she remembered she'd told McCabe she would lock up for the night. She hadn't known when she left for Dana's house that she was staying for dinner.

She parked and went inside. Everyone but the dispatcher and the hotline operator would be gone home or out on patrol. Laney waved at the two officers manning the phones. Usually there would only be the dispatcher but help was needed with the incoming hotline calls. She locked her office and McCabe's and then headed back out. Another wave to the officers and she was out the door.

As she walked toward her vehicle the mayor waved to her. He was just coming from his office, which was next door to City Hall. At one time, she was told, the mayor's office had taken up the biggest part of City Hall but then the shop next door became available and it was purchased to relocate the mayor and his staff into more suitable accommodations.

Laney stalled on the sidewalk. "Hey, Mayor Jessup. You're working late tonight."

"You appear to be as well, Deputy Holt."

Thomas Jessup was the one person who balked at Laney's title and salary. He'd thought it was foolish to have a chief and a deputy chief over only a handful of officers. McCabe had insisted he couldn't expect a highly qualified detective to take the job without some incentive. The City Council had ignored the mayor's suggestion and sided with the chief. Laney wasn't sure the mayor realized she knew the disagreeable details. He was always friendly to her which she hoped meant he had accepted the circumstances.

"I thought I might catch Chief McCabe for an update."

Laney found it strange that McCabe hadn't given an update to Jessup. He certainly kept the City Council up to speed. Maybe there was bad blood between the two. "He had a late meeting." This was a lie but she figured she owed it to McCabe to cover for him. "I'm happy to bring you up to speed, if you'd like."

Jessup scrutinized her for a moment, almost as if he sensed she was lying. At thirty-six he wasn't that much older than her. Laney suspected a good portion of his salary went on clothes since he was a walking, talking definition of the term clotheshorse. Never a dark hair out of place, and green eyes that seemed to look right through you. The man was handsome and single but not at all her type even if she were in the market.

"I would appreciate that. Shall be go into my office?"

Laney glanced around the sidewalk. Since it was nearly seven there was no one along this particular block, all the businesses were closed. "We can talk here. There's not that much you don't already know. We've re-interviewed the victim's employees."

He held up a hand. "I'm sorry. Can we not call her the victim? I'd prefer to use her name. It's more personal and we need to keep this close to our hearts."

"Of course. Habit." She resisted the urge to sigh. "We've also spoken to a number of Sylvia's friends and, certainly, her family. We're still waiting on the lab to give us the results of the evidence collected at the scene. Nothing useful on the hotline yet. And that's pretty much it." She had no intention of bringing up all that money that was currently at the lab for fingerprint processing. McCabe may or may not have told him, that was the chief's call. She couldn't see any reason the mayor needed to know just now.

Jessup nodded. "Well, it certainly sounds like you're covering all the bases. Hopefully you'll have more soon. We should have another press conference on Monday. I'll arrange it for the same time, around five."

No pressure. Laney felt confident McCabe would be thrilled to hear this news. "I'll let the chief know."

"Good night, Deputy Holt."

"Night, sir."

Laney loaded up and drove straight home. She thought about calling McCabe and telling him about the press conference but decided to wait until morning. Why ruin his night, too?

To her surprise, his Bronco was parked in her driveway. Laney parked next to him and climbed out. She checked her cell to make sure he hadn't called. No missed calls.

"I didn't call," he announced.

She walked around the front of her car and looked up, saw him sitting at the top of the steps on her front porch. "Well, hello to you, too."

Hitting the lock button on her fob, she climbed the steps and sat down beside him. He held a pint of Wild Turkey, it was somewhere in the vicinity of half empty. She'd only seen him drink that stuff one other time. This was not a good sign.

"Did you open that before or after you got behind the wheel?"

"*After* I parked myself right here on your porch," he said, his tongue a little thick.

"I see."

"I bought the Wild Turkey to split with you but I just kept waiting and waiting and you didn't show so I started the party without you."

"You know I hate Wild Turkey." She reached for the bottle, took a swig. Made a face at the burn. So not palatable to a casual drinker like herself. She shuddered.

"I know. I figured there would be more for me this way."

She laughed, couldn't help herself. "Let's go inside. You should eat."

He swayed a bit when he stood. Laney resisted the urge to steady him. Instead, she moved to the door and unlocked it. He joined her, his gait a little off.

"You should eat, too."

"I already ate." Laney opened the door and flipped on a light. Pearl pranced toward her, tail twitching.

McCabe followed her inside and closed the door. "Oh, that's what took you so long to get home."

"Yep."

Laney went to the refrigerator. Pearl shot one look at

the chief and followed Laney. With a little digging, Laney found some cheese. She prepared a plate of crackers and cheese and a can of Vienna sausages she found in the pantry. They might have been in there from the previous owner but the expiration date was still in the future. She took the plate and a bottle of water to her boss where he'd crashed on the sofa.

"Eat all of this." She placed the bottle on the table next to the sofa. "Drink the water." She snagged the Wild Turkey and left it on the counter. "I'll be right back."

He gave her a crooked salute and set in on the cheese.

In her bedroom, she put her badge and weapon away. Toed off her shoes and peeled out of her jacket. She would change after she showered, but first she needed to find out what was going on with McCabe.

He was still plugging away at the goods on the plate when she returned. Pearl was now parked on the coffee table watching him. Wild Turkey in hand, Laney sat down beside him. She took another sip, closed the lid tight and parked the whiskey on the sofa between them.

"So, what's going on?" she asked.

He finished off a sausage. Washed it down with water. "Vernon told me to get off his property." He shrugged as she reached for a chunk of cheese. "There were a few other choice words, but those are irrelevant."

Laney told him about what Dana had agreed to do and about Vinn's slip in grades that came a few months after the Bradshaws dropped off of Sparkle's client list. She also, reluctantly, told him about her conversation with the mayor. That was when he bypassed the water and returned to the Wild Turkey.

"Getting shitfaced is not going to help the situation," she reminded him.

He set the mostly empty plate aside and downed

another swallow of whiskey. "Maybe not, but at least I won't care."

Laney reached for the bottle, despite the voice warning her she would be sorry, and knocked back another slug. The chief was fully aware of her buried demons—the ones that haunted her dreams every night. And one of these days she was going to know about his.

The man had demons and this murder had resurrected them the same way it had Laney's.

CHAPTER ELEVEN

Saturday, October 6

Vinn should have told the police everything.

Rage burned inside him. But he was a coward. A damned coward.

He flopped over onto his back, stared at the ceiling fan. He could smell breakfast. His mother always made pancakes on Saturday mornings, but he didn't want to get up. He just wanted to lie here and pretend nothing had changed. Pretend that his parents were still the same loving people they'd been before.

But nothing would ever be the same.

Sylvia was dead.

Vinn closed his eyes and fought the tears. He would not cry for her! He wouldn't. She lied to him. Lied. Lied. Lied.

He was glad she was dead.

His eyes flew open and his fingers fisted in the sheets.

No, no, no. That wasn't true. He wasn't glad. It shouldn't have happened. He should have…

What could he have done differently?

Begged her to stop? Begged her not to ruin his life?

She would have laughed and told him to grow up the same way she did when he yelled at her in that stupid parking lot. Someone had seen them and told the police. Now he was a suspect or something.

He hadn't wanted anyone to know. His lips trembled as more damned tears slid from his eyes. He really didn't. It was private. No one was supposed to ever, ever know. But now they would.

The whole world would know before this was over.

There had never been a murder in Shutter Lake. That cop—that woman, Laney Holt—was a big time detective in Los Angeles. She wasn't a drunk like the chief. She would know how to figure everything out.

She would find the truth and then it would be the end of everything.

He had to do something. He couldn't let that happen.

But what?

One person was already dead.

His lips quivered. Sylvia was dead.

Was he going to kill someone else to try and stop the inevitable?

He couldn't do that.

Fear gnawed at him. He was a coward. If he hadn't been a coward—if he hadn't been so blind and selfish—none of this would have happened and Sylvia would still be alive.

He had believed her when she told him not to worry that everything would be okay. He shouldn't have believed her.

He should have killed the person who started all this.

That's what he should have done.

But he couldn't do that to his mother. She had been hurt enough.

Six months ago...

She laughed and laughed and laughed.

Vinn had sat crossed legged on her living room floor and watched. He loved the way Sylvia laughed. She was so beautiful. How could any girl—woman, he reminded himself—be so beautiful? He loved his mother and thought she was beautiful, but it was different with Sylvia. His feelings for her were way different.

He smiled as she wiped her eyes. He liked that he made her laugh even when they were supposed to be working.

"Okay," she said, finally catching her breath. "We have to finish this. It's due tomorrow, right?"

He nodded. "I turned in the report today but I need the charts for my presentation tomorrow."

"One more and we've got it."

His presentation was about entrepreneurship. Sylvia had designed and launched her own business at eighteen—just a year older than he was right now. By the time she was twenty-one she had added six employees and moved into an office downtown. She was the perfect example, in his opinion, of a successful entrepreneur.

"There you go!" She stared at the words she'd written on the page. NEVER GIVE UP! "That gives you six charts." She looked at him, her eyes glittering with happiness. She was the happiest person he knew.

He nodded. "That's enough."

Pounding on her front door made her jump. She made a face. "I guess I should see who that is before they beat the door down."

Vinn watched her get up and tiptoe to the door. She was so beauti-

ful. His whole body burned to touch her, but he couldn't do that. They were friends. He couldn't risk ruining their friendship by making a stupid pass. But man he wanted to. He wanted to touch her all over.

She turned back to him after checking the peephole and hurried back over to where he sat, her bare feet soundless on the floor. She whispered, "It's your mom. Will she be mad you're here?"

He made a face. "Definitely."

"Hide in my bedroom," she whispered. "I'm sure whatever she needs it'll only take a moment."

Vinn grabbed the charts they had made and rushed into her bedroom. He would turn them into a PowerPoint presentation when he got home and then he was done.

He pushed the door almost completely closed but left a crack so he could listen to whatever his mother had to say. It wasn't because he was afraid his mother would get the wrong idea about him being at Sylvia's. She had no idea about his feelings for Sylvia. He just didn't want his mom to know he was doing his presentation on Sylvia instead of on his dad.

He couldn't hear everything they were saying but his mom sounded upset. Vinn tried to focus but he couldn't help looking back at Sylvia's bed. Unable to stop himself, he sneaked over and leaned down to sniff her pillow. Smelled just like her. Man, he wanted to pick it up and hug it. He bit his lip and looked around at her private space. He'd never been in her room. Her closet door was standing open, but he'd better not go in there. He was already hard just from talking to her and being in the same room with her. He couldn't help himself, he knelt down and sniffed her sheets. God, they smelled so good. He laid his cheek there and imagined staring into her eyes as they lay facing each other in bed.

His mother and Sylvia sounded deep in conversation so he unzipped his jeans and reached inside with one hand. He couldn't help himself. He was about to bust. He closed his eyes and thought of pushing into Sylvia, of hearing her call his name. He'd barely touched himself when he came. His eyes jerked open and he shoved himself back into his jeans. Embarrassed he tried to make sure he didn't have any on the front of his jeans. His hand was sticky with it. What was he going to do? He couldn't risk going into the bathroom and turning on the water. He reached under the edge of the bed and swiped his hand on the rug. Sylvia wouldn't notice it there. Maybe it would fade away before she ever cleaned under her bed.

He was such a loser!

Feeling like an idiot, he eased to his feet and backed away from the bed. Stupid. Stupid.

The voices in the other room got even louder and he sneaked back to the door. What the hell were they arguing about? He opened the door a little wider and listened.

"Don't you ever come back to my house!"

Vinn frowned at his mother's mean voice. She was never mean like that.

"Mrs. Bradshaw——"

"Never, I said," his mother snarled, cutting Sylvia off.

Why would his mom be mad at Sylvia? He didn't like that she was being so mean.

"You stay away from my family or you'll be sorry, do you hear me?"

"This is way out of control," Sylvia said, still pretty calm. "You should leave now, Mrs. Bradshaw."

"I'm telling you and you'd better listen," his mom screamed. "If you go near my family again, I will make you wish you hadn't."

That was the day Vinn should have done something, but he hadn't. He had allowed Sylvia to convince him that his mom was just overreacting and that everything would be fine. Once his mom was gone, Sylvia had come to him and promised him that it was nothing. She had hugged him so hard. He'd felt her breasts pressed against him and he'd melted. He'd believed everything she said.

But she'd lied.

She'd lied and now she was dead.

He should have killed her that day instead of waiting.

And now there was no way to change what was done.

CHAPTER TWELVE

You killed me.

Laney turned away from the boy lying face down on the ground. She couldn't bear to look. Couldn't bear to face what she knew she would see when she turned him over. Blood oozed from beneath his body, soaking into the gray sweatshirt.

His blue jeans were ragged and hanging below his waist…one leg was twisted at an odd angle.

He was dead.

In the dream she reached toward him, cupped her right hand over his shoulder and turned him onto his back. His mouth was open, his face frozen in a mask of surprise but it was his eyes that crushed her. His dead eyes stared into hers. The eyes of a twelve-year-old boy.

You killed me.

Laney bolted upright. She couldn't breathe. Couldn't get air past the constriction in her throat.

A dream. Just a dream.

She struggled to catch her breath. Closed her eyes and waited for her heart to slow its frantic pounding. Pearl raised her head, stared at her in question. Laney reached out and patted her.

Another deep breath, then another. Finally, Laney pushed back the covers and shoved her hair out of her eyes. It had been more than a year since she'd suffered with those nightmares. She went to the bathroom and washed her face. A million years could pass and the fact would never change. She had shot and killed that kid. No matter that he had shot her partner and that he was readying to take a shot at her, she would never be able to forgive herself.

"Suck it up." She couldn't drag through life feeling sorry for herself.

She brushed her teeth, rounded up a pair of jeans and a pullover sweater since it was Saturday. The top item on her agenda today was re-interviewing the Bradshaws. McCabe had said that Vernon Bradshaw refused to talk, practically kicked him off his property.

One shoe on and one off, Laney hesitated. Damn. McCabe was on her sofa. He'd been far too drunk to drive home last night. To tell the truth she had likely been beyond the legal limit as well so she'd insisted he sleep on her sofa.

Damn, damn, damn.

After tugging on the other shoe, she ran a brush through her hair and braced to face the music. McCabe was never a happy camper before ten in the morning. That she'd ordered him around last night would no doubt make his attitude all the more foul.

Well, he shouldn't have shown up at her door if he wasn't prepared for the consequences.

In the two years they had worked together this was the first time she'd had to take care of him twice in one week —less than a week actually. She wasn't the only one feeling the pressure of this investigation. Cutting him some slack, it would be tougher for him. He'd known Sylvia her whole life and, the fact is, the Shutter Lake Police Department had never investigated a murder before.

This was just hard all the way around.

The instant she opened her bedroom door the smell of coffee filled her lungs. So, he was up. No sign of him in the living room. She drifted into the kitchen and found him staring out the window over the sink, mug of coffee in hand.

"Good morning."

He turned around. "It could be worse."

A day's beard growth mixed with the bloodshot eyes and the slightly wrinkled shirt almost made him appear vulnerable. That was one thing she'd never jotted under the mental list of impressions he'd made since hiring her.

"Coffee smells good." She poured herself a cup. "You think there's any chance we can change Mr. Bradshaw's mind?" Laney wasn't entirely sure she was ready to point a finger at Vinn Bradshaw but there was something going on that related to Sylvia and it was intense. If nothing else, they needed to rule the boy out so as not to waste time. Sylvia's murder was more than forty-eight hours old. Every hour that passed at this point lessened the likelihood of finding her killer.

"I don't think so. We can try arranging an interview with the attorney present but I'm thinking that's going to get us nowhere."

"You know this family." Laney leaned against the counter. Pearl rubbed against her legs. "What are the chances that Vinn Bradshaw could commit an up close murder like this? Is he even strong enough to have over-powered Sylvia? She was fit. Worked out often. The kid is clean. No drugs. He's on the basketball team so you know they drug test him. I can see him hyped up on some drug and going crazy, but he doesn't do drugs."

McCabe scrubbed a hand over the stubble on his chin. "I just can't see him doing it, which is why it bugs the hell out of me that Vernon won't let us clear this up with another interview."

"Unless Mr. Bradshaw has something to hide. The Bradshaws fired Sylvia. Maybe Vinn's mom caught daddy messing around. That could be why he felt so confident allowing us to talk to Vinn at school. He knew Vinn had nothing to hide, but things didn't go the way he expected." Laney shook her head. "Whether he killed her or not, the kid knows something."

"I'll call the attorney and tell him we need to talk to the whole family. Maybe the kid will open up despite what the lawyer or his parents say. It was clear he wanted to. He's got something to say, he's just afraid to say it."

Laney had come to the same conclusion. "I've thought some more about what Shonda Reed said. You know, about the trip Sylvia was planning to Venezuela. The lab is going through her laptop, they may find she was searching human trafficking. It's possible she was on a mission to find the missing girl who worked for her a few months back." She shrugged. "I can't see how that would have gotten her killed unless she poked the wrong bear and it sniffed its way to her house."

"That's a long shot, for sure." McCabe poured himself another coffee. "But we'll see what the lab has to say."

Silence lingered for about a minute. Laney suspected he was as deep in thought as she was. Two days and not one damned bit closer to uncovering what happened to Sylvia Cole. Pearl looked up and voiced her own opinion. Laney reached down and gave her a stroke, then rounded up her kitty breakfast.

"I'm sorry for showing up at your door and imposing on you last night."

Laney reached for her mug once more and met his gaze. "I didn't have plans anyway."

"That's not the point. There are things I need to get under control. I'm aware, but it's easier said than done."

"We all have our demons." She thought about the nightmare that had awakened her. "Sometimes they're hard to shake."

"Well, I've allowed this one to eat at me for a long time. I should be moving on rather than looking back."

"Sometimes they follow you." Laney had tried hard to outrun hers, didn't work.

Their gazes held, a kind of understanding passing between them. There were some things that were better left unsaid.

McCabe reached for his cell. Took a call.

Laney grabbed a cup of yogurt from the fridge. What she really wanted was a poppy-seed bagel. Maybe she'd drop by The Grind in a couple of hours. She intended to stay on top of Ikard until he was honest with her. What was it with all these people and their secrets?

McCabe ended the call and tucked his cell back onto his belt. "That was Lott Delaney. We've got a crowd gathered outside City Hall. He's doing what he can to answer their questions. They want to know why we haven't solved this murder yet." He set his mug in the sink. "I'm thinking I might need backup."

Laney tossed the empty yogurt container into the trash bin. "I'll be right behind you."

She had known this was coming. Who knew it would take two whole days?

Approximately thirty people were gathered outside City Hall. Laney parked in her usual spot and met McCabe in front of his Bronco.

"Our esteemed mayor is standing right beside Zion Cole," he said, clearly frustrated.

McCabe had shaved on the way here. Apparently he carried an electric shaver in his vehicle as well as keeping one in his locker. Eyes looked a little clearer. He no longer looked exactly like a guy who had a hangover. More like one who'd worked all night and hadn't gotten a wink of sleep.

"Might as well hear what they have to say." Laney squared her shoulders and headed toward the waiting crowd. McCabe walked beside her.

"Chief McCabe," Jessup said. "Deputy Holt. I arrived at my office this morning and found this concerned group of citizens waiting for your arrival. I've been doing all I could to bring them up to speed."

"Thank you, Mayor." McCabe took a place in front of the crowd, braced his hands on his hips and said, "Good morning. I'm sure you're all here for the same thing." He glanced at Zion Cole. "You want answers."

"My wife wants to know when we can bury our daughter, Chief," Cole spoke first. "I've called you three times in the past two days and I've gotten the same answer every time."

"Zion, there is no one who wants to get this done more than me. But we're at the mercy of the coroner's office. I'm hopeful we'll have news next week. Until then, there's just nothing I can do. I wish that wasn't the case, but it is."

Frustration rumbled through the crowd. A reporter from the Sacramento paper stepped forward. "Based on Mayor Jessup's briefing, it sounds as if your department doesn't have the first suspect. Have you considered calling in help from a more experienced agency? Perhaps Shutter Lake isn't prepared for this kind of investigation."

Laney tensed.

"Actually," McCabe said, "Deputy Holt was a homicide detective with a stellar solve rate before joining us in Shutter Lake. She's a top-notch investigator. We are doing all that can possibly be done. The Nevada County Crime Scene Unit is providing support."

"Shutter Lake is a small, tight community," another reporter piped up, "how are the citizens handling the idea that they likely have a killer in their midst?"

The crowd rumbled with uneasiness. Several citizens Laney recognized spoke up, echoing those same concerns.

Another twenty minutes of answering questions and McCabe urged the folks to go on about their days with the knowledge that Shuttle Lake PD had the investigation well in hand.

Jessup and Cole followed them into City Hall.

McCabe jerked his head toward his office when Laney would have detoured to her own. She wanted to groan, but she understood. He needed her to have his back in all this. After all, she was the one with the experience. Her experience was in the field, not in the political part of the investigation.

"Chief, I've been fielding endless calls about how slow this investigation is moving," Jessup complained. "We really need to see some results by the time we have the press conference on Monday."

"One of Sylvia's girls told me," Zion spoke up, "that Sylvia still took care of Troy Duval's home personally. All the others are afraid of him. For that matter, none of us really knows him. I believe you should look into him."

"I interviewed Mr. Duval," Laney spoke up. "Sylvia took care of his home personally because she considered him a good friend. Mr. Duval is very ill and frail. He wouldn't have had the physical strength to harm your daughter, Mr. Cole."

"How can you be sure?" Cole demanded. "Are you a doctor as well as a former homicide detective?"

"Zion," McCabe stepped in, "I know you're hurting and I understand that you're upset, but there's no need to go after the people who are trying to help."

Cole exhaled a big breath. "I apologize, Deputy Holt. I'm certain your instincts are well honed when it comes to sizing up someone like Troy Duval." He shook his head. "I just want to know what happened to my baby." Tears shone in his eyes. "I want whoever did this found. I want it over so my wife and I can grieve in peace."

"We're doing everything we can," McCabe repeated the assurance he'd given the crowd that had assembled outside.

"Zion," Jessup reached out, patted his arm, "we should go now and let them do what needs to be done. I'm certain the chief will have news for us by Monday." Jessup sent a look at the chief—one that challenged him to make that happen. To Cole he said, "Come on. Let's get you home."

When the two men had gone, McCabe dropped into the chair behind his desk. "Tell me what to do, Holt. We've got just over forty-eight hours to figure this out before we have a riot—one prompted by the victim's father and the mayor, I suspect—on our hands."

Laney perched on the edge of the chair in front of his desk. "First of all, we can't make something out of nothing, but we can give the entire community something to think about. We can walk them through the steps of what we have been doing. Rather than saying we're doing all we can, tell them *what* we're doing."

He blew out a breath of exasperation. "I can do that. I guess I should have today."

Laney smiled. "Then you wouldn't have had any bones to throw them on Monday."

"Good point."

"Second," she went on, "we rattle the Bradshaw cage. It's the best lead we have."

McCabe shook his head. "I can't get right with the idea that the kid did this."

"He probably didn't," Laney agreed. "But he knows something. And right now we just need to learn whatever it is he knows. That's the thing about murder investigations. It's the little things that no one believes are important that usually make all the difference."

"One rattle coming up." McCabe picked up the phone on his desk and made the call to the attorney.

The Bradshaw home sat behind an iron gate at the end of a long paved driveway. The grand house was surrounded by woods and elegant landscaping. Inside, the great room was made for entertaining with soaring ceilings and floor space that went from the front wall of the home to the back.

Vernon, Connie and Vinn sat on the sofa. Their attorney, Morris Barton, sat in a chair next to the sofa. Laney and McCabe took the sofa facing the Bradshaws. A seven or eight foot wood coffee table sat between them, like the border between two warring countries.

"You may ask whatever you like," Barton announced, "and we reserve the right to pass on anything we feel is out of line or inappropriate."

McCabe nodded to Laney and she began. "Vinn, when we last spoke you seemed very upset about something

Sylvia had done. I believe you said she'd lied to you. Will you tell us what happened to upset you so?"

Vinn opened his mouth, but Barton spoke first. "We feel as if you've explored that avenue well enough, Deputy Holt. Perhaps you'd like to ask something else."

"Vinn," she said again, "you seemed very angry with your father in our last meeting. Was he somehow involved in whatever it was that Sylvia did to upset you?"

The attorney held up his hand again. "You are just determined to beat that dead horse, Deputy."

Laney wanted to tell him that the only dead horse she wanted to beat was him. Damn. "Mr. Bradshaw." She turned her attention to the patriarch of the family. "What was your relationship with Sylvia Cole?"

"Until a few months ago, she was an employee of my wife's. She cleaned our house once each week. Beyond that, I knew her as a resident of Shutter Lake. I've been to parties at her family's home, as her family has been to parties at mine. Everyone knows everyone in Shutter Lake, Deputy. We all have close relationships."

While he spoke Laney watched Vinn's face. He practically sneered at the man. Oh yeah. Daddy had done something to upset the son.

"What about you, Mrs. Bradshaw?" Laney shifted her attention to Connie Bradshaw. "What was your relationship with Sylvia?"

The attorney held up his hand again. "I believe Mr. Bradshaw has already answered that question sufficiently."

"Not really," Laney argued. "He said Sylvia was an employee of his wife. So I'm asking his wife about the relationship. I'm certain she can tell us why she decided to fire Sylvia. After all those years of being satisfied with her work, why would you suddenly fire her?"

Connie stared at Laney for a moment before she spoke. "She stole some of my jewelry."

This time Vinn's mouth actually dropped open.

Both the mother and the father were lying.

"Did you report this theft?" Laney asked.

"We are close friends with Zion and Yolanda," Vernon Bradshaw began.

"The question is for Mrs. Bradshaw," Laney told him.

"We didn't want to cause any hard feelings with Yolanda and Zion so we let it go," Connie said, "Sylvia and I parted amicably."

Again Vinn stared at his mother, clearly stunned by her words. Good boy.

Laney exchanged a look with McCabe. They had discussed how this would go. He gave Laney the go ahead to give the Bradshaws something to think about. But she wanted to be sure he hadn't changed his mind. He nodded.

Well, all right then.

"If you have no more questions," the attorney was saying.

Laney shook her head. "No more questions, but there is something I'd like to say to the Bradshaws." She stared directly at the attorney. "And to you."

He turned up a hand indicating that she should proceed. "Be my guest, Deputy."

Laney shifted her attention to the three seated on the sofa. "Vinn was involved with Sylvia in some manner."

Barton lifted his hand and Laney shook her head. "You agreed to hear me out, sir."

"Let her have her say," Vernon Bradshaw said. "Let's just see how foolish the Shutter Lake PD really is."

"I know you were," Laney said to Vinn, her gaze pressed against his. "I have yet another witness who saw you have a tense exchange with her. Whatever your parents and your lawyer over here tell you, we know this. It's only a matter of time before we know the exact nature of that relationship." Laney glanced first at Connie, then at Vernon, but her attention resettled on Vinn. The son was the weak link. "We also know there was trouble between your mother and Sylvia. She wouldn't have fired her otherwise. Do I believe she fired Sylvia for stealing? Not for a second. Sylvia was wealthy in her own right. She didn't need your mother's jewelry."

All three stared at her with faces of stone, but the fear in their eyes was clear.

"Are you quite finished, Deputy Holt?" Barton's patience was at an end.

"I am." Laney stood. "You think about what I said, Vinn, because I will find the truth, one way or another."

Beside her, McCabe nodded. "Have a nice day."

They were outside in his Bronco before he spoke.

"You pushed the boy hard." He started the engine and turned the vehicle around.

"He's the only chance we've got of getting the truth."

McCabe glanced at her. "You're good, Holt. Really good."

"You said that already, Chief." Laney laughed. "If you keep it up, I'm going to expect a raise."

He braked at the end of the drive. "I mean that I couldn't do this without you. You've got the best cop instincts I've had the privilege of encountering. And, for the third time, you are damned good."

"I appreciate it, Chief. Let's just hope I'm good enough."

CHAPTER THIRTEEN

At two o'clock on Saturday afternoon downtown Shutter Lake was crowded with pedestrians. Folks who lived in town walked to restaurants and pubs for late lunches or early afternoon drinks. The Wine & Cheese House was particularly busy on Saturdays. Laney, Dana, Julia and Ana often gathered there for girls' night. Laney had taken her mother there when she visited back in the summer. Speaking of her mother, Laney really should go home for Christmas this year. She'd missed the past two.

She watched out the front window from City Hall. She should have called it a day half an hour ago. McCabe had told her to take the afternoon off, let the interview with the Bradshaws stew with the rest of the pieces of this investigation simmering in her head. He was right. It was time to mull it all over and decide on the best next move.

McCabe was in the process of re-interviewing four of Vinn Bradshaw's closest friends. The fathers had all said they were happy to allow their boys to talk to him as long as he was alone. Evidently word about Laney's newest interview with Vinn had already hit the grapevine. Small town gossip lines were fast and notoriously influential. No one would look at Laney the same after this investigation.

The people who had welcomed her so graciously wouldn't be so gracious anymore.

Nothing she could do about that. Finding Sylvia Cole's killer was far more important than a few ruffled feathers.

She hadn't really expected this easy, laid back way of life to last. She should have known that life in Shutter Lake was too pleasant to be true. A laugh bubbled into her throat when she recalled that back when she'd described the place to her mother and her sister she'd compared her new hometown to Stepford, Connecticut, the fictitious town in that movie about the perfect wives in the perfect community.

Considering the age of the men who had founded this town, she wondered how many had been thinking of that old movie when they created their idyllic new community.

"No more Wild Turkey for you, Holt," she muttered to herself.

Laney walked back to dispatch and gave a nod to the two officers fielding hotline calls. She sat down at the small conference table in the center of the room to review the stack of printed out notes about each call. Any notes on relevant calls would be routed directly to Laney and McCabe, but it never hurt to look over the rest of what came in. She'd done so twice already this week. McCabe reviewed the notes everyday and she was reasonably sure he would have let her know about anything important.

As she skimmed the pages, she thought again about the cash in Sylvia Cole's hidden safe. One former prostitute on staff did not an escort service make, but the money had to have come from somewhere. As for drugs, no one had been busted for drugs beyond the marijuana that a couple of middle school students had been growing among their mother's flowers in her garden nearly a year ago.

A rap at the door drew Laney's attention. Dana Perkins stood in the open doorway. She waved and showed Laney the file folder in her hand.

Laney left the call lists and joined the principal at the door. "Hey. Did you recall something else that might be useful to our investigation?"

"I'm not sure, but I thought you might want to see this project." She indicated the file.

"Let's go to my office."

Laney led the way back to her office and gestured toward the only chair besides the one behind her desk. "I'm glad you've been thinking about all this." She reached for the file. "As difficult as it is to keep the murder in front of you, you never know when the next thing that comes to mind will be the one that makes the difference."

She nodded. "I've been thinking along those lines. The project is one our juniors did right after the school year started. The teacher asked her students to write a report on entrepreneurship. They were to choose someone who started their own business and saw success."

Laney opened the file and saw the title and author on the first page. *A Sparkling Success by Vinn Bradshaw.*

The first page after the title page showed a photo of Sylvia Cole. Her smile was beautiful, playful. Page after page lauded her ingenuity and success. Vinn Bradshaw was totally smitten with the woman.

"I was discussing your idea with some of my most trusted colleagues and one of them reminded me about this project." She exhaled a heavy sigh. "I know this all looks as if Vinn had some sort of obsession with Sylvia but I just can't see him that way. He has never given any of his teachers reason to believe he would harm a fly, much less a person."

"Is it all right if I keep this for a few days?" Laney asked rather than giving her the agreement she wanted about Vinn. Sometimes good people did bad things.

"Of course." She shook her head. "I am so torn about this. I feel incredibly guilty presenting material that casts him in a bad light."

"Don't feel guilty, Dana." Laney placed the file on her desk. "Putting all you believe about him aside, if Vinn did harm Sylvia, it's better that this awful secret is discovered now so that he can receive the kind of help he needs. It's very possible there's an underlying mental disorder."

"You're right." Her face showed the relief she felt at the idea. "The most important thing here is that we do the right thing, for Sylvia and for Vinn."

"This was the right step in that direction."

When Dana was gone, Laney decided she needed another look around the victim's home. Maybe they'd missed something or maybe something that had appeared innocuous before would look different considering all that they now knew.

Which wasn't a hell of a lot.

She'd driven across town and made the turn onto Olive Tree Lane when her cell vibrated against her waist. She tugged it free, thinking it would be McCabe with something he'd learned from Vinn Bradshaw's friends.

The number wasn't McCabe's. "Deputy Holt," she said in greeting.

"Deputy, this is Troy Duval."

He was one person she hadn't expected to hear from again. "Mr. Duval, I hope you're doing well." It occurred to her that he might be ill and need some assistance.

Without Sylvia, he likely didn't have anyone else to call as of yet.

"I'm fine, thank you. But something has been troubling me and I really feel as if I need to share it with you."

Laney parked in Sylvia Cole's driveway. "Do you need me to come to your house?"

Anticipation lit in her veins. He appeared to have been closer to Sylvia than any of the other friends and associates she had interviewed, with the exception of Fernandez and possibly Vinn Bradshaw.

"That's not necessary. I'm certain you're very busy with the investigation. I can share my concerns with you now, if you have the time."

Laney shut off the engine. "I do, yes, sir."

"You see, I watched my beautiful wife suffer greatly at the hands of powerful, greedy men. I didn't want to see that happen to Sylvia. If the nightmare I lived could somehow be helpful to her, then perhaps it was not for nothing."

Laney kept quiet, allowed him to tell his story without any interruptions.

"So I gave her some advice several years ago. Advice she heeded well. Perhaps too well."

When his silence lingered, Laney couldn't help herself. "What sort of advice, Mr. Duval?"

"Sylvia was under the mistaken impression that Shutter Lake was a boring, nothing ever happens place. She looked at the people she had known her whole life and saw them as quiet, harmless beings who never crossed the street without a crosswalk or traffic light."

Laney had made those same sorts of conclusions when she first moved to Shutter Lake. Today wasn't the first time she'd likened the eerily serene place to the fictional Stepford, but the town was far closer to the tranquil paradise it appeared to be than most other towns. Still, there was no denying that bottom line: wherever humans collected in one place there would be some measure of evil. It simply wasn't possible to have one without the other. Unfortunately.

"I warned her that she was being naïve. I suppose it was my bitterness talking but it was the truth, still is. There are secrets here the same as any other town. I advised Sylvia to learn all the secrets she could. To watch the people for whom she provided housecleaning services. To learn their secrets in order to be armed if the need ever arose. Knowledge is power, Deputy Holt. I'm certain you know this better than most."

There was no denying his point. "Knowledge is a very powerful tool," she agreed. "Why would you be concerned about urging Sylvia to arm herself with knowledge?"

He'd already given part of the answer, but she wanted to hear the rest.

"She made several comments over the months and years after that day. At first it was surprise or shock at how wrong she had been about certain people. She never said who or what had shocked her. I remember feeling great pride that I had helped to open her eyes. But then she stopped mentioning the secrets she had discovered. Not that she specified what those secrets were, more a comment about being surprised, as I said. But over the past two years she has on several occasions thanked me for helping her see how naïve she once was. She went so far as to say my advice had changed her whole life. She wouldn't elaborate further, but after she was murdered I began to worry she had gotten in over her head with this business of secrets."

"So far, Mr. Duval, we haven't found any reason to believe that's the case." Even as Laney said the words she thought of the money they'd found.

If Sylvia had been blackmailing her clients that would certainly explain all that cash. But it was difficult to believe not one single person broke and allowed some reference to the blackmail to slip. How many people were involved? Her first thought was of the Bradshaws.

"Perhaps it's nothing. I may have read more into her comments than she meant, but I had to tell you if there was any chance blackmail might be the motive for her murder."

"You have my word that I will pursue this avenue to the best of my ability, Mr. Duval. And, please, if you think of anything else, call me."

He assured Laney he would and the call ended.

She stared up at the house. "What the hell were you up to, Sylvia?"

The street was quiet as Laney emerged from her car. Then, things were always quiet in Shutter Lake. She climbed the steps to Sylvia's deck. At the front door, she tugged on gloves before pulling loose the posted warning that the property was currently considered a crime scene.

Inside, she closed and locked the door behind her. No point risking a reporter showing up and walking right on in like he or she owned the place. The house was cool inside, cool and dark. Laney flipped the switch next to the door and half a dozen overhead can lights shed a glow over the expansive living area.

"Where did you keep all your secrets, Sylvia?"

Laney moved to the far side of the living room or den, whatever Sylvia considered the space where the sofa, chairs and television called home. Shelving lined one wall. Laney started with the lower shelves since they were readily accessible. Rather than just looking around and beneath things, she opened every single book. Fanned through the pages. Any sort of container or vase had already been inspected but she inspected them again. She pulled out the penlight she carried and peered into each opening of any piece that had one. Once she reached the shelf at eye level, she went in search of a ladder or stepstool.

The stepstool she found in the kitchen wasn't tall enough so a trip to the garage was necessary. The garage was fairly clean. Not much to look at in there and the Crime Scene Unit had gone over her vehicle thoroughly. Nothing in there either. Ladder in hand she returned to the living room.

Slowly but surely she reached the top shelf and came up empty handed for her trouble. Then she moved on to the rest of the room. Since the ladder was handy, she first checked behind every framed photo and piece of artwork hanging on the walls. She moved every table, checked inside and under every drawer, under rugs, inside the heating and cooling vents. She even stuck her head in the fireplace and looked up in the chimney.

Once the living and dining areas were done, she moved to the kitchen. She poked around inside any open package of cereal or crackers or whatever. Drawers, cabinets, under and behind and inside every single thing. Nothing.

She moved on to the stove and then the fridge. A half empty bottle of wine, cheese, grapes and several other fruits were tucked into the see-thru drawers. On the top shelf in the fridge was a box from Batter Up Bakery filled with cupcakes. Laney's mouth watered. Heidi Udall made great cupcakes.

"Don't even think about it." She closed the fridge door and moved on.

Since the guest room and hall bath would be quicker, she walked to that end of the house next and executed the same sort of search in those rooms. Within half an hour she was moving toward the master bedroom. That room would take some time.

The bed linens were at the lab and the mattress had been removed from the bedsprings for a thorough inspection and then returned. There was nothing under the bed. Not even an odd shoe.

Lastly, she retrieved the ladder and ventured into the closet. From the very top shelves she thoroughly searched and made her way downward. She went through every hanging and folded garment once more. Inspected every pocket, every fold. Same with the lingerie. And she found exactly what she'd found last time—nothing.

Laney returned the ladder to the garage and decided to check the exterior of the house. It had already been given a once over for ruling out forced entry. This time she intended to look for anything, including a hidey-hole.

First, she walked all the way around the house, checked the outside of the windows and all the doors. When she reached the windows of the master bedroom, she paused. The redwood siding was in pristine condition. No deferred maintenance around this place. She crouched down and looked more closely at the siding directly under the windows of this room. There were a couple of scuffs in the wood finish, almost as if someone had climbed into or out of the window.

Since she couldn't reach the window from outside, she went back into the master bedroom and checked the locks. Both the locks were in the proper position. Well, hell. The windows being locked blew that theory.

Unless, one of the locks didn't work.

Laney pushed up on first one and then the other. The first window wouldn't budge, but the second one shifted, going upward as if it wasn't locked at all. She leaned out the window and sure enough the scuffmarks lined up. She closely scrutinized the window frame, particularly the sill. The window was as old as the house, forty or fifty years, and metal. Her gaze lit on what appeared to be a small piece of skin. Anticipation roaring in her veins, she rushed to the kitchen and found a sandwich bag and then she located a tissue. As carefully as possible she removed the piece of skin and tucked tissue and all into the bag.

If she was really lucky DNA could be extracted from the skin. If it matched the semen, it was possible Sylvia's lover and her murderer were one in the same. Laney closed and locked the window for the good it would do considering the lock was broken.

But why would the person who murdered Sylvia—someone she knew and invited into her home and with whom she possibly had sex—feel compelled to exit through a bedroom window? Not to mention the scuffmarks gave the impression of climbing in.

Just one more detail that left her with more questions and no answers.

CHAPTER FOURTEEN

Sunday, October 7

Laney stepped up to the counter to place her order. Nolan Ikard stared at her expectantly. No hello. No casual, flirty attitude. This was not like the man who usually took her order at The Grind.

"I'm going to splurge," Laney said. "I'll have your classic Chai Tea Latte and an apple cinnamon bagel with honey."

"Coming up." Ikard said this like a man on his way to the gallows rather than as a happy entrepreneur grateful for the busy morning filling his till.

Laney had purposely waited until almost nine to come in just to make sure she missed the before church crowd. She'd wanted a more one-on-one encounter with Ikard. Another of his part time baristas, this one a young guy— probably a student, was busy cleaning up and restocking after the morning rush.

Laney watched as he went through the steps to fill her order. If that wasn't enough sugar to get her motor running this morning, she was beyond resurrection. After revisiting the crime scene last evening she had driven to the lab to hand deliver the evidence she'd discovered. Hours later, she had still been pacing the floor. Couldn't sleep. She kept replaying the possible scenarios. Each piece of evidence—such as it was—circled around in her head. The faces of the persons of interest—particularly Vinn Bradshaw and Nolan Ikard—kept popping into the mix.

Troy Duval was worried because he had encouraged Sylvia to learn as many secrets as possible. And maybe she had. Maybe that's what the cash stacked in that safe in her closet was about. But the person who killed her wasn't just an angry individual—perhaps one being blackmailed, he was an intimate. Someone to whom she felt close enough to open her door to him while wearing a nightshirt. Someone who startled her so that she hardly fought back as he choked her to death with his hands. No bruises on the body, save her neck, to indicate a struggle.

Unfortunately, not with his bare hands since no fingerprints had been found on her skin. That was the part that suggested premeditation. At this point, she and McCabe hadn't talked in depth about the possibility the killer had arrived at Sylvia's house with murdering her in mind.

But the meager evidence they had could not be ignored.

Ikard bagged her bagel and she considered the long sleeved tee covering his arms. He wore jeans the same as he always did. Whoever had climbed in or out that window had scraped an arm or a leg, maybe a bare chest. Did he have a mark somewhere on his lean body? Or Vinn. Laney could see him going out that window.

"That'll be twelve fifty-six."

Laney blinked and brought her attention back to the here and now, her gaze locking on Ikard's. "Someone had sex with Sylvia the night she was murdered."

He flinched.

"Would you be willing to provide a DNA sample, Nolan? Just to clear yourself. Everyone knows the two of you had something going."

He held up his hands, backed up a step. "I don't know what you're talking about."

"Sex, Nolan." Laney didn't bother glancing behind her to see if anyone else had walked into the coffee shop. She would have heard the bell jingle if someone had. The other barista had disappeared into the back for supplies or to take a break. It was just the two of them. Time to pour on a little pressure. "I'm talking about sex. You and Sylvia were involved which makes you a person of interest in her murder. Do you want to clear yourself or are we going to have to do it for you? Whatever was between you and Sylvia, you need me on your side, Nolan. Trust me."

He shook his head. "You're wrong. That's all I have to say. It's on the house this morning. Have a nice day, Deputy."

He turned and disappeared through the door marked Employees Only.

Well, that went exactly as she'd planned.

Laney picked up her coffee and the bag of goodies and walked out of the shop. She sat down on one of the benches between The Grind and Batter Up Bakery. She might as well infuse all this sugar into her veins. Eventually she would need to bring McCabe up to speed on her chat with Ikard.

The part that bugged the crap out of her was that if Vinn Bradshaw and Nolan Ikard had nothing to hide, why not just be honest and up front? Furthermore, if that was the case, they had no idea that their subterfuge was doing nothing but muddying the water and hindering the investigation. She wanted to shake them both.

She couldn't see either one of them as the killer but her instincts had been wrong before. Images of a kid running in the darkness attempted to intrude and she pushed them away.

"Well, good morning, Deputy Holt."

Laney looked up, startled. Heidi Udall stood over her. She hadn't heard the bakery door open or the bell that certainly jingled as it did.

"Good morning." She stuffed a final bite of bagel into her mouth.

"I had to come in today to ready the wedding cake for this afternoon's ceremony. The Brewsters' only daughter is getting married. The cake is so huge I had to call in my backup baker, Sheena." She dabbed at her forehead with the back of her hand. "This is going to be a hell of a wedding cake!"

Laney glanced toward the bakery, noted the royal blue hair of Sheena Appleton. She was far younger than Heidi and lived in Grass Valley. As best Laney recalled she had only seen her working in the bakery a couple of times. The young woman was eccentric, to say the least. Laney dredged up a smile. "I think there's been a wedding every Sunday for the past two months."

"I'm telling you. They've kept me busy." Heidi sat down beside Laney. "How's the investigation going? I'm hearing all sorts of rumors."

"Investigations like this always move too slow," Laney said without really answering the question. "What rumors are you hearing?"

Heidi leaned back and crossed her arms over her ample chest. She was a large woman in girth but not so tall. Her hair was gray with white streaks. She wore it down and was rarely seen without her baker's hat. Her round face generally wore a friendly smile. Laney, as well as most of the residents of Shutter Lake, was well aware Heidi and Ikard despised each other. Heidi felt his bagels and pastries encroached on her sovereign territory as the town baker. She often threatened to start opening for breakfast and serving designer coffees and decadent sweets.

The war was a well-known one. The question was, did the baker know anything about the barista beyond their fierce competition.

"Oh my," Heidi said, "the rumors are a bit crude."

Laney laughed. "I'm from L.A. You couldn't shock me if you tried."

"Well, first I heard that all sorts of sex toys were found in her bedroom. And…" She leaned close to Laney. "I also heard that she was running a little escort service with all those pretty employees of hers."

"Interesting," Laney said before taking a sip of her latte.

"They are all so pretty." Heidi made a not so polite harrumph. "I wouldn't doubt it. And that Sylvia. Poor thing was a gold digger, that's for sure."

"A gold digger?" Laney wadded her bag and tossed it into the trash bin a yard or so away. Nailed it. She gave herself a mental fist pump. She turned back to the baker. "I don't know what you mean?"

"I heard," Heidi glanced around to make sure no one was near, "that she was out to cheat people out of every dollar she could by whatever means necessary."

Laney frowned, an exaggerated expression. "Really?"

Heidi pressed her fingers to her lips for a moment. "No one else told you this?"

"No." Laney shook her head. "Do you mean like stealing or blackmail? Something underhanded like that?"

"Oh my." Her hand went to her chest then in mock horror. "I hate to speak ill of the dead, but that's what I heard. Yes. I hope it's just a nasty rumor. Sylvia seemed like a nice girl."

"You were one of her clients, weren't you?"

The baker's face flushed just a little. "I was, yes. In fact I was one of her first clients. She was fresh out of high school and running around trying to drum up business. I saw a little of myself in her so I jumped on the bandwagon." She smiled, her gaze distant as if she were remembering those days. "It's hard to believe someone murdered her." She leaned close again. "I heard she ate something that made her sick and the killer took advantage of her weakness." Her face furrowed with worry. "Is that true? Are you allowed to say how she was murdered?"

"I'm afraid I'm not at liberty to say at this time."

"I'm sure these are just rumors. When people are afraid they tend to take the slightest little thing and make something out of it. Really all they want are answers."

"We're doing all we can," Laney assured her. "Hopefully we'll have some answers soon. But you shouldn't believe the rumors you hear. Most of the time there's no foundation for the gossip. As you say, just folks trying to figure this thing out."

"You're right, I guess. I didn't really believe all that nonsense. Besides, Sylvia was very smart. She wouldn't have been foolish enough to get in over her head. And if, for some reason, she had, she would have gone straight to her daddy to get it taken care of. Zion Cole would never allow his little girl to feel threatened. I'd sure hate to be whoever did this. Zion is not the kind of man you want to cross."

Laney considered the other woman for a moment. "I imagine any father would be out for blood if someone murdered his child."

Heidi shrugged. "I'm sure. But you've only been here for two years, Deputy Holt. You don't know these people the way I do." She exhaled a big breath. "In any event, Shutter Lake will never be the same now. Murder changes everything."

Later, Laney simply couldn't shake the baker's comment.

In two years this was the first time Laney had been made to feel like an outsider. Maybe, as Udall said, she didn't know the people in Shutter Lake as well as a lifetime resident. But surely McCabe would have told her if Zion Cole was the sort of man who put fear in other people. If that was the case, there could be a whole different scenario for Sylvia's murder.

"Damn you, McCabe."

It wasn't that Laney accepted whatever the nosy baker said as gospel, but the possibility that there was some semblance of truth in the mix infuriated her. She pointed her vehicle in the direction of McCabe's house. Chances were he was nursing a hangover. Something else she was about fed up with. She immediately felt contrite at the thought. She was angry, that was all.

Her cell vibrated on the console. She snatched it up, hoping maybe it would be McCabe and that for once she would be wrong about his condition. Not McCabe. A Sacramento number.

"Deputy Chief Holt."

"Hey, Laney, this is Harry Morgan. I tried to reach Chief McCabe but I couldn't. I knew you guys were waiting on these results."

"Thank you for calling me." Morgan was a senior analyst at the crime lab. He wasn't the only one who hadn't been able to reach the chief. "I'm headed to McCabe's house now so I can pass along whatever you have for us."

"Great. Okay, well you know these things usually take a good deal longer, but apparently Zion Cole has some powerful connections. The boss put a rush on all the testing. So, here we go. First, the easy stuff. The fingerprints McCabe passed along from the tabletop were found among those lifted from the victim's home."

Damn. Vinn Bradshaw had been in Sylvia's house. Not a complete surprise, but not what Laney had wanted to hear.

"Next up, whoever left the semen on the sheets is the same person who used the toothbrush. He's also the same person who had sex with the victim before she died. The specimens belong to a male but he is not in any database to which we have access."

Laney had figured as much. Sylvia was too smart to get tangled up with a known criminal. Still, she was undeniably uber-independent but she had a lover—a buddy as Shonda Reed said.

Vinn Bradshaw had no criminal record so of course he wouldn't be in a DNA database.

"What about the evidence I dropped off last night?"

"I'm working on it now."

"Thanks, Harry. I really appreciate the update."

"There's one other thing."

Laney made the turn onto McCabe's road. "What's that?"

"There was another semen specimen collected. The note says it came from the rug in the bedroom. This one is not in the database either and it's not a match to the semen on the sheets."

Well, well, Sylvia had herself two lovers.

"Thanks, Harry. I appreciate the call."

Laney parked next to the chief's Bronco, got out and went to the front door. As hard as she could she banged on it. If he was in there still piled up at this hour, she hoped he had a raging headache and that her pounding sounded like shotgun blasts in his brain.

Another round of pounding was required before he opened the door. He squinted at the daylight, his face a mask of agony. "Even a cop should get a break on Sunday."

Her frustration escalating, Laney pushed past him and into the house. When he'd closed the door and turned around she let him have it. "Sylvia Cole is dead. You think her murderer gives one shit that it's Sunday? You think her parents care that it's Sunday? We have a job to do and it doesn't get put on hold because of the day of the week. We talked about how badly I need you for this investigation. I need you at one hundred percent, McCabe."

He stared at the floor, ran a hand through his hair. "Yeah, okay. I had a bad night."

"Well, join the crowd. Let me make you some coffee. We have stuff to talk about."

Properly humbled, he followed her into the kitchen. "I heard from Parker last night."

"The coroner called you and you didn't bother to tell me?" Now she was even more pissed. "Are we a team or what?"

"It's not like he told me anything we didn't already know. She was manually strangled—the whole town knows that part. She had been drinking. Blood alcohol level was a little higher than the legal limit for driving, but she wasn't falling down drunk. No other drugs so far. He confirmed there was nothing under her nails so she didn't scratch her attacker. There are still a few tests to come—as you know some take longer than others—but for now, we can assume there was nothing but the alcohol. No food in her stomach. She'd had sex just before she was murdered." His gaze settled on Laney's. "Looks like the son of a bitch killed her just a little while after."

The idea made Laney sick to her stomach but it was the way these things worked far too often. "I went back to the house and had a look around."

She brought him up to speed on the unlocked window and the new potential evidence she took to the lab.

"I guess I wasn't the only one keeping secrets." He leaned a hip against the counter and stared at her with the accusation ringing between them.

"You got me there." She exhaled a burst of frustrated air and punched the brew button on the drip machine. Another deep breath and she felt reasonably calm. "On the way here Harry Morgan called. Whoever had sex with her is the same person who used the extra toothbrush she kept in the bathroom."

His eyebrows went up. "So he was a regular."

She nodded. "But he wasn't the only one. The semen found on the rug near the bed wasn't the same as what was on the sheets."

He scrubbed a hand over the stubble on his face. "And I'll wager that neither one is in the database."

"Bingo."

McCabe shook his head. "This is going to get even uglier."

"You should keep an eye on her father. I hear he pressed for speedy testing and I also heard that he isn't a man you want to cross."

McCabe looked away. "Whether he is or not, the bastard we're trying to find killed his daughter. I'd have to be a fool not to recognize that Zion is going to want revenge as well as justice."

"Good to know we're on the same page." Laney considered the clothes he wore, the same ones from yesterday. She passed him a cup of coffee. "You should change. We have doors to knock on."

He accepted the coffee and disappeared to do as she'd ordered. Laney shook her head at the mound of dishes in the sink. While she waited she loaded the dishwasher and started it. She picked up the beer cans and pizza boxes in the living room and took them to the trash bin by the garage. She needed to work off some of this frustration. She'd lost it with him and she shouldn't have.

But this case—the total lack of forward momentum— was making her crazy.

By the time McCabe showed his face again she had the place in reasonably good order. And he looked halfway human.

"You didn't need to do all that."

"I needed to stay busy."

"So who's cage do you want to rattle?"

"Nolan Ikard's. I want a DNA sample. I think he's the regular."

"All right." McCabe reached for his service revolver and his cell, both of which lay on the coffee table. "We'll need something more to persuade him."

"Or just a coffee mug he drank from. Maybe a water bottle."

"Are you suggesting we bring him in for questioning and then give him refreshments?"

"Exactly."

McCabe's cell vibrated and he glanced at the screen then answered it. "McCabe."

He listened for a minute then said, "We'll be right there, sir."

Laney braced for more bad news.

"That was Quentin Windermere. He says the girl, Kristina Sharapova, the Russian exchange student who's been living with them since July, wants to talk to us."

The Windermeres lived on the same street as Sylvia but all the way at the end on a grand estate.

"Dana Perkins said Sharapova and Vinn Bradshaw are close friends."

"Let's go."

"I'll drive," Laney told him.

He grunted but didn't argue.

When they'd loaded up and headed out, he stared out the window as if lost in thought but then he spoke. "This is Shutter Lake's first murder but it's not the first evil incident."

Laney waited for him to go on but he didn't say more.

"What evil incident?" She was aware of a few burglaries, the occasional bar room brawl.

"It was a long time ago." He shook his head. "Not relevant."

Funny thing was his tone made it sound entirely relevant.

CHAPTER FIFTEEN

The Windermere residence sat at the very end of Olive Tree Lane. The large gated property had its own lake and a massive Tahoe-style mansion. Laney parked in front of the grand house.

McCabe touched her arm as she shut off the engine. "Don't try any of your slick L.A. questioning tactics on Mr. Windermere. He's some sort of genius. A mathematician or something like that. He helped create the system for browsing the Deep Web. He's not like us, Holt."

Laney smiled. "Thanks. I'll keep that in mind. Why don't you take the lead? They know you, maybe they'll feel more comfortable talking to you. I'll question the girl."

He nodded. "Sounds like a plan."

As soon as they were finished here Laney wanted to set her other plan in motion as well. She intended to call both Nolan Ikard and Vinn Bradshaw to City Hall for interviews. She didn't care one way or the other if they both showed up with attorneys as long as she managed to get them to drink from a water bottle or coffee cup. Another of her L.A. tricks, as McCabe would say. She called it discreet evidence collection.

The front door opened as they walked up onto the porch. Quentin Windermere nodded to McCabe. "Thank you for coming so quickly. Kristina is inconsolable."

Laney followed the older man beyond the entry hall and the music room, complete with a distinguished baby grand piano, to the great room that extended along the back of the house overlooking the private lake. Quentin Windermere was tall and broad shouldered. He carried himself well, dressed like a 1960's hippie who had grown into his wealth. Top of the line designer jeans that were well worn, probably purchased that way, and a blue cotton classic Henley pullover. His feet were bare and his gray hair was styled in one of those spikey cuts.

Katherine Windermere sat on the sofa next to the young girl, Kristina Sharapova. Sharapova was the student Dana had mentioned. Vinn Bradshaw was close to her, the principal had said. Her head was bowed as if she were afraid, her long dark hair concealing her face. Katherine kept one arm around her shoulders. Like her husband, the older woman went for comfort in her attire. She wore a cotton tunic with her worn soft jeans. Slim bare feet were adorned with red toenails. Her long gray hair hung in a loose braid. These two appeared exactly like the quintessential retired California couple.

"Please," Mr. Windermere said, "make yourselves comfortable. Would you like coffee or tea?"

Laney declined, as did McCabe. The only thing she wanted to do at the moment was dive into questions about Vinn. But she had to hold back, see what the girl offered first.

"This morning," Katherine Windermere began, "Kristina broke down over breakfast. She cried for nearly an hour before we convinced her to share whatever was troubling her."

"Kristina," Mr. Windermere said, "you need to tell Chief McCabe and Deputy Holt what you told Katherine and me this morning. It's very important and I assure you that you are not in any sort of trouble."

The girl peeked at Laney beyond the curtain of long hair. Her fingers rolled and picked at the wad of tissues in her hand.

Laney took that as her cue. "Kristina, you shouldn't be afraid to tell us anything. It's our job to keep you safe."

"She explained to us," Katherine said, "that in her village it was considered a very bad thing to speak to the police. You could be taken away from your family and never seen again."

"That won't happen here, Kristina," Laney assured her. "We only want to help you." When the girl still didn't look up, Laney went on, "I understand you're friends with Vinn."

Sharapova's head came up then, her face was red from crying, her dark eyes were round with fear.

Laney gave her a reassuring smile. "Vinn is a very nice young man. He's very upset by Sylvia's death. She was a friend of his, too." She might be stretching things here so she left it at that.

"He was hurt by her," Kristina said, her voice shaky but unyielding. "She was not as nice as you believe."

"Did you hear or see something about Sylvia?" McCabe asked gently. "Whatever it is, you can tell us."

The girl's hair swung back and forth as she shook her head. "I only know that she hurt Vinn deeply. He trusted her."

"How did she do that, Kristina?"

She shrugged. "He wouldn't say. He only said not to trust her."

Laney and McCabe exchanged a glance but waited for her to go on.

"The night she died," Kristina hesitated, exhaled a big breath, "I was out walking."

Anticipation seared through Laney. She clenched her jaw to prevent hurling questions at the girl.

"It was late." She glanced at Mrs. Windermere. "I wasn't supposed to be out of the house, but I needed some fresh air."

When she fell silent, Laney asked, "Did you walk past Sylvia's house?"

She nodded. "It was when I was coming back, past her house, that I saw someone."

Laney held her breath.

"He came from around the back of her house and ran down the road."

"Did you see who it was?" McCabe asked.

She shook her head. "It was too dark. But he was tall and fast. He ran really fast."

She broke down. Mrs. Windermere passed her another handful of tissues. Laney gave her a moment to compose herself once more.

"Kristina, I need you to think carefully and tell me which end of Sylvia's house you saw this man run from. Was it the end going back toward your house or the other one?"

She dabbed at her eyes, seemed to mull over the question. Eventually, she said, "The one on this end."

Bingo. Sylvia's bedroom was on this end of her house. The window and the scuffmarks would explain why the fleeing man had come from that end of the house.

"Think back, Kristina," McCabe said, "before you saw

this man, did you hear any voices? Maybe someone shouting? Or a slamming door? Any sound at all?"

She hesitated a moment, then said, "No. It was so quiet. That's why he startled me. I wasn't expecting anyone to come rushing from the direction of her house."

"Were there any lights on in her house?" Laney asked.

Kristina frowned. "Yes, in the window by the front door. I guess the living room."

The light from that window would never have reached the yard much less the street. There were no streetlights that far out of town. Laney had reviewed the weather from that night, the cloud cover had almost hidden the moon. No wonder the girl hadn't gotten a look at the guy.

"Is there any possibility that he saw you?" McCabe asked.

She shook her head again. "I was on the other side of the road. With all the trees I don't think he could see me. I wouldn't have seen him except he was running so his shoes were making that sound on the pavement. I heard him first. Then I saw him streak past."

"Kristina," Laney said, "I know this is extremely difficult, but I need you to think very carefully before you answer this question."

She nodded.

"Was the person you saw running from Sylvia's house Vinn?"

Her head shook almost frantically. "No. No. It wasn't Vinn."

"How can you be so certain?" Laney pressed. "You said it was dark. You couldn't see him well enough to identify him."

She didn't answer for a moment but her eyes were wide with worry or fear.

"Kristina," Mr. Windermere said, "you don't need to

be afraid. Whatever your answer, we'll be okay. We've already discussed that you shouldn't have been away from the house at such a late hour, particularly so far away. But we're not going to punish you for telling the truth. We'll only hope you won't do this again."

She nodded, more tears slipping down her cheeks. "I walked to the other end of Olive Tree Lane to meet up with Vinn. We talked and…" She glanced at Mrs. Windermere. "We kissed. But that's all. We didn't do anything wrong."

The older woman patted her knee. "We have complete faith in you, Kristina. We don't believe you would do anything wrong. Kissing a boy you like isn't wrong."

"You can't tell his parents," she cried. "His parents are too hard on him. They wouldn't understand."

"Kristina," Laney said, drawing her attention, "did Vinn tell you why he was so upset with Sylvia?"

She shook her head. "He wouldn't talk about it. He has been so upset since the murder but he won't talk to me at all."

"I'm sure he'll come around when he's had time to recover from the shock," Mrs. Windermere offered.

"Kristina, where did this man who ran from Sylvia's house go? Did he disappear into the woods or did he go back the way you had come? Toward town?" From Sylvia's house, it was about four miles back into town. Unless the man left a vehicle somewhere, he had a hell of a walk.

Or run. Laney ran five or so miles most nights. Maybe this guy did, too.

The frown that marred the girl's face told Laney she hadn't considered that question until now.

"I don't know. He just kept running. I never heard a car or anything like that. Just the sound of his shoes on the road." She stilled, then nodded. "He ran and ran and ran."

"One more question, Kristina," McCabe said. "Did you see a car or truck, maybe an SUV in Sylvia's driveway?"

The driveway was visible from the street. Laney mentally crossed her fingers.

"Only her white car. That was when I first saw him, when he ran past her white car. I froze. Afraid to run or to say anything."

The man probably didn't see her. And if it wasn't Vinn —if her alibi for him could be trusted—there was only one other person it could be, in Laney's opinion.

Nolan Ikard.

"Thank you, Kristina," Laney said, "for telling us about what you saw. Sylvia's parents are devastated by what happened to their daughter. They want her killer found as quickly as possible and coming forward with what you saw may very well help us make that happen."

The girl nodded though she didn't appear particularly happy. She was worried about Vinn.

"If you think of anything else," Laney added, "please call us." She handed her card to Kristina.

She nodded again.

McCabe stood. "We really appreciate your help," he said to the Windermeres.

Mr. Windermere walked them to the door. "We'll try and keep the communication open. If she remembers anything else we'll let you know."

McCabe shook his hand. Laney did the same.

Loading into her vehicle, she went straight to the point. "We need Ikard's DNA. My money is on him."

McCabe fastened his seatbelt. "I think you're right. Let's pick him up."

As Laney pulled away from the Windermere home, McCabe's cell vibrated.

"McCabe."

She maneuvered her vehicle along Olive Tree Lane, slowing as they passed Sylvia's house. Why would Ikard murder Sylvia? Jealousy? He seemed too damned laid back to work up enough energy to murder her over another man.

Did he have a secret she had learned? Maybe he killed her to keep his secret.

McCabe ended the call and put his phone away. "Nolan Ikard will have to wait. That was dispatch. Vinn Bradshaw is at City Hall. He says ne needs to talk to us."

So maybe the big break they had been waiting for was about to happen.

Laney paused at the front entrance of City Hall. Beyond the glass she spotted Vinn Bradshaw seated all alone on a bench in the lobby. When he spotted the boy, McCabe groaned. "You know we'll have to call his parents before we can talk to him."

Laney turned to her boss, "You call his parents. I'll go keep him company while we wait."

"Don't question him," McCabe warned as he reached for his cell.

She held up her hands. "Got it."

Laney entered the building. The whoosh of the door closing behind her drew Vinn's attention in her direction. He shot to his feet.

She gestured for him to sit back down. "No need to get up, Vinn. Let's sit for a while."

"I need to tell you something, Deputy Holt."

Damn but she wanted to hear it. "We have to wait and

do this all official and everything." She had a feeling if she told the kid they needed to wait for his parents he would balk. Clearly he was on a rebellious path. Meeting his girl-friend in the middle of the night. Talking back to his father in front of the cops and his principal. Whatever was going on with Vinn, he wasn't behaving like the good kid everyone thought him to be.

At the moment he looked nervous. One leg wouldn't be still, the knee bouncing. His hands were clutched in his lap, fingers twisting. He was scared.

In spite of herself, Laney had to say something. "That was a great report you did on Sylvia Cole's business. Ms. Perkins showed it to me."

His knee stopped bouncing and he stared at Laney. "Why did she show you the report?"

"She wanted me to know you and Sylvia were really good friends."

He looked away. "Ms. Perkins is wrong."

"A person can still be your friend even when they disap-point you or make you angry." Laney was pushing the envelope here. She needed to shut up and wait like the chief told her.

A shrug lifted one skinny shoulder. "Whatever."

Thankfully, McCabe arrived and prevented Laney from pushing the boundaries any farther.

Vinn shot to his feet again. "I have something to tell you, Chief."

He held up his hands to stop the kid before he could go on. "We have to do this by the book, Vinn. Deputy Holt will get you set up in the interview room and then we'll hear what you have to say, understand?"

He nodded. "Yeah, sure."

The anticipation was killing Laney, but she did as McCabe said. She escorted Vinn to the conference room that also served as an interview room when the need arose.

"I'll get you a bottle of water," she offered, seizing the opportunity to snag his DNA.

He muttered an okay and she went to the break room and grabbed a bottle for him and for herself. If he saw her drinking he was far more likely to follow her example.

She returned to the interview room, placed his bottle in front of him and sat down. She opened her own bottle and took a long swig. She had to take another couple of sips before Vinn followed suit.

Good boy.

By the time McCabe appeared, Laney was getting antsy. The Bradshaws and their attorney followed the chief into the room.

Vinn stood and pointed at his parents. "I'm not talking with them in here."

The parents and the attorney started talking at once. Urging the boy to keep quiet. To discuss with the attorney what he had to say before he told the police.

Vinn refused. He turned to McCabe. "I want them out of here."

Laney was more than happy to let the chief handle this hornet's nest.

"Vinn, I'm afraid due to your age, we can't listen to anything you say without either one of your parents present or your attorney."

"The attorney, then." He glared at his father. "I want you out of here." He looked to his mother then. "You, too, Mom."

A few minutes of discussion was required but the attorney finally convinced the parents to leave the room. Laney's nerves were jumping by the time she, the chief and the attorney settled around the table.

McCabe placed a small audio recorder on the table. "We'll be recording your statement, Vinn."

"Good." He nodded. "I want you to."

Laney's instincts were roaring. As much as she wanted to hear what the kid had to say, something was off. Way off.

McCabe stated the date and time along with the names of those present for the recording. Then he looked to Laney to take it from there.

"Vinn, you came to City Hall and stated you wanted to talk to the chief and to me. Before you say anything, I need to advise you of your rights."

While the attorney looked on and made the occasional note, Laney recited the Miranda Warning.

"Do you understand your rights as I have explained them, Vinn?"

He nodded.

"I need you to answer aloud, please."

"Yes." He cleared his throat. "I understand my rights. Now can I talk?"

"By all means," Laney said, giving him the floor.

"You can close your investigation into Sylvia Cole's murder," he announced.

In the chair next to her, Laney felt McCabe tense.

"Why do you believe we can close our investigation, Vinn?" he asked.

He extended his arms across the table, turned up his wrists. "Because I'm here to confess." He looked straight at Laney as he spoke. "I killed Sylvia. She made me angry. I lost control, and I killed her."

Read on for a sneak peek at what happens next in Shutter Lake! And please help an author by leaving a review!

SNEAK PEEK

Enjoy this Sneak Peek of the next BREAKDOWN book,
so many secrets, by Vicki Hinze ©2018

Chapter One

Monday, October 8

Five days.

Impossible to believe but that's all it had taken for the idyllic vision of Shutter Lake, California, lauded by *Country Living* as the most perfect town in all of America, to prove perfection is a façade and all the safety and security sought and found in it had been an illusion.

One murder. Illusion shattered.

One murder, and so many secrets…

A shiver crept up Dr. Dana Perkins's backbone. She stiffened against it, determined to reclaim her sense of security here. At the deli counter inside Stacked, a block off downtown's main square, she ordered a grilled chicken sandwich with a side salad and a bottle of Evian berry-flavored water, then glanced over to the cluster of two-dozen tables. About half-full. A lot of people were having a late lunch today.

Dana took a table surrounded by empties then settled in and reached for a sheaf of papers from her tote. She had been through the school records at least a dozen times, but maybe in the sandwich shop, she would be more objective, gain some new insight, and see something she had missed.

Oh, but she needed to be certain she hadn't missed anything. After Phoenix, to retain her sanity she had to be absolutely certain she hadn't missed any warning sign.

There had to be a reason this year's best and brightest student had confessed to murder. Some logical, rational reason that Vinn Bradshaw, gifted future nanotechnologist, studious, popular basketball player, who exhibited nothing short of fantastic leadership skills, confessed. Vinn could not have killed anyone much less a prominent Shutter Lake founder's daughter like Sylvia Cole.

Nolan Ikard, about thirty, tall and lean with sandy blond hair and a handsome man's confident swagger, paused at her table. Nolan owned The Grind, a coffee shop sharing a common wall with Stacked that Dana frequented every morning on her walk from home to the school.

"How's our favorite principal?" Nolan asked. "Things settling down any at S.L.S.?"

Many students, current and former, referred to Shutter Lake School as S.L.S. "Getting better," she said because it was expected and not because it was true. "The students are still rattled, but then aren't we all?"

He nodded and avoided her eyes, his own gold-flecked

ones clouded and troubled. "Guess the kids won't settle down until their parents do. Maybe we will all get back to normal soon."

"Maybe we will." Dana smiled.

He walked on to his favorite table beside hers and next to the front window. How many times in the last year had she seen him staring out that window as if he had lost his last friend? She'd been tempted often to ask if he was okay, or to offer to listen if he needed to talk, but something had held her back. She couldn't say what, but she always followed her instinctive urges on things like that. In his case, she hoped she didn't live to regret it.

A waitress Dana didn't recognize delivered her order. She must be from Grass Valley. She hadn't been one of Dana's students.

That was a perk of being principal of a school with three-hundred students. You knew them, and they knew you. The other items on the waitress's tray were Nolan's. Cuban sandwich and a side of slaw. A hint of citrus, garlic and a splash of white wine gave the mustard on his sandwich a distinct scent that set her mouth to watering. It smelled spicy and tart, interesting. It smelled great.

When the waitress placed his food on the small square table in front of him, Nolan barely glanced at her. That piqued Dana's curiosity and fired a red-flag warning too bold to ignore. Nolan Ikard not flirting with an eligible woman? Normally, he'd flirt with a lamppost. Oh, not offensive flirting, just friendly flirting. It was as natural to him as breathing. But not today.

Apparently his perfect façade of Shutter Lake also had shattered—and Dana certainly shouldn't make too much of it. Everyone in the community seemed disturbed and wary and disillusioned these days.

Shifting her thoughts to her work, she studied the details in Vinn's files and nibbled at her food, wishing she'd dared to order Nolan's hot and spicy Cuban. Stacked made the best sandwiches and slaw in the tri-county area, but with Dana's stomach acting up since Vinn's confession, she didn't dare to risk eating anything not mild.

About a third of the way through the teachers' observation notes, she spotted Kristina Sharapova's name. Her image sprang to mind: long dark hair and eyes, pale skin and a mischievous smile that was nothing short of infectious because it was so rare. Kristina bent toward being serious, which was normal for a teenage Russian exchange student. They competed so fiercely for the chance to come to Shutter Lake to study.

Thanks to the wealthy and childless benefactors, the Windermeres, there were always foreign exchange students at Shutter Lake School. Attending there was an amazing opportunity for all the students really. A group of the most gifted professionals in the world in science, medicine, and industry designed and created the nearly self-sustaining community and they often shared their vast pool of knowledge and expertise with the students.

Dana was proud of the program she and Mayor Thomas Jessup had created. In two short years, its success rate at preparing knowledgeable, socially mature and motivated graduates had surpassed expectations and her wildest dreams.

On Kristina's first day with them, she had been like a fish out of water. Who wouldn't be? Strange school, no familiar friends or faces. Living in a strange country and speaking a foreign language. But Vinn Bradshaw had picked up on her uneasiness. Without prompting, he'd taken her under his wing and helped her fit in. They were, according to the file observation note, good friends.

Dana too had been wrong about that. She reached into her tote for a pen, accidentally pulled out a large Ziploc bag, and smiled to herself. Every teacher she'd ever known carried a waterproof bag in her handbag or tote. Old habits die hard. Stuffing the frosted bag back in, she snagged the pen and then scribbled a new note on a page she had labeled "Things to tell Laney."

Laney Holt was the Deputy Chief of Police and lead investigator on Sylvia Cole's murder case. A beautiful young blond who favored long hair and ponytails over short red hair like Dana's and, guessing, a year or two younger than Dana's thirty-four. *Not just friends.* She added the note to the list.

Laney Holt breezed by Dana's table with an order of fries and a bottle of flavored water then dropped into a seat at Nolan's table.

He didn't look happy to see her.

Gauging by the level look she laid on him, she wasn't happy to see him either. "I still need your DNA," Laney told Nolan.

Dana didn't deliberately listen but, when people seated three feet from you talk, unless you cotton-stuff your ears, you can't help overhearing their conversation.

"Why?" Surprise flickered through Nolan's eyes. "You've got your killer. Word's out all over the lake Vinn Bradshaw confessed."

Laney finished chewing a fry, swallowed and then sipped from her water bottle. "Paperwork," she said.

"You want my blood to check off a box to make sure your case sticks?" He shot her a resent-laced look of disgust.

"Exactly." Her lips curved in a smile that never touched her eyes.

"And?" He pushed.

"And a witness saw a man fitting your description running away from Sylvia Cole's house the night she was murdered. Chief McCabe wants no loose ends."

"I don't care what McCabe wants." Nolan frowned. "You clowns get a description that fits half the men around here and naturally you come after me."

Laney's voice stiffened, but her expression appeared as calm as it had before the tension between them rocketed. "This *clown* is trying to eliminate you as a possibility, Ikard." She tilted her head. "Wait a second. Are you saying it was you?"

Silence.

Laney bit into another fry, let the silence stretch, yawn, settle. Finally, she asked, "Did Sylvia tell you she was planning a vacation to Venezuela?"

Dana's heart rate sped. She kept her nose down and her gaze focused on her papers. One night after Yoga class at the Community Gathering Center, Sylvia had told Dana about that trip. A few weeks ago, Sylvia had even come to Dana's cottage to see her mask collection. They'd talked for a few hours. Before Phoenix and coming to Shutter Lake, Dana had loved to travel. She'd spent her summers exploring, including three trips to Venezuela.

Nolan answered Laney. "Sylvia didn't tell me anything about any vacation anywhere. We didn't talk much."

"So was it you—running away from her house that night?"

"No."

As if she hadn't heard him, Laney went on. "There's one thing I don't understand." She polished off her last fry, took a long draw on her water. "Why did you climb out of the window instead of leaving through the door?"

No answer.

She dusted the salt from her fingertips with a paper

napkin. "I get that Shutter Lake is a small community and maybe you two didn't want to broadcast your intimate relationship, but...the window?"

"I told you." Nolan's jaw tightened and he leaned forward in his seat. "Sylvia and I were friends back in school. It was a long time ago. You knew her. That woman had no interest in a relationship with me or anyone else. She was as independent as people come."

"Just in it for the sex. Got it." Not one to cower, Laney leaned in, spoke to him nearly nose to nose. "So you went out the window to show her you're independent, too. Uh-huh. Well, that makes perfect sense." Her sarcasm couldn't be missed. She scooted back her seat then stood up. "You've got twenty-four hours to come to the station and handle that DNA sample."

"Or what?" he said, his voice a sharp and cutting tone Dana had never before heard him utter. "No. You know what? Forget it." He glared up at Laney. "You want my DNA, get with my lawyer."

"You have a lawyer?" Laney bared her teeth in a would-be smile. "Does he have a name?"

"Morris Barton."

Her smile turned genuine. "Ah, here's a tip. You might want to start looking for a replacement. Barton is Vinn's lawyer." She turned. "Twenty-four hours, Ikard."

Nolan didn't draw a breath until Laney exited the door of Stacked and stepped out onto the sidewalk.

Muttering and agitated, he finished his meal.

Dana ordered a cup of coffee, studied her papers with her mind whirling, and waited.

Finally, Nolan left and, when the door closed behind him, she phoned Laney. "You need to come back to Stacked right away."

"What's wrong?"

"Nothing. Just get back here as fast as you can." Dana caught the waitress two steps away from Nolan's table. "Don't touch anything."

The startled waitress jerked back and darted a worried look at Dana. "What?"

"Don't touch anything on that table." Dana hated this. But Vinn's whole future could ride on what happened next, and no one was going to rob him of it. Not on her watch.

Scant minutes later, Laney entered Stacked and rushed straight over to Dana. "What's wrong?"

"I told you on the phone, nothing is wrong."

Laney stilled, parked a hand on her hip. "Then why am I here, Dana?"

"On TV, I saw an investigator going through a person of interest's trash. The can wasn't on his property, it was at the curb, waiting for the collector. He said once trash is abandoned, it's legal for him to look in it for evidence. Is that true?"

"Well, yes," Laney said, looking a little bewildered. "If it can be proven that it wasn't contaminated."

Dana rubbed an itch at her earlobe, tugging it. "Meaning, no one else touched the abandoned trash?"

"Right."

Dana nodded toward Nolan's table. "Well, Nolan Ikard abandoned his trash at that table and left Stacked. His DNA is on that fork and glass."

Laney's eyes narrowed. "Has anyone—"

Dana cut in. "The waitress delivered his food, but since he abandoned the trash, the table and departed, no one else has come near that table. It's untouched," Dana said. "I'll swear to it."

Laney nodded, appreciation lighting her eyes. "Let me grab an evidence bag."

Dana pulled the Ziploc from her purse. "Here you go."

A smile curled Laney's lips. "How long has that puppy been in your purse?"

Good question. One Dana couldn't answer. "Not a clue."

"Best use mine, then." Laney retrieved a bag and gathered the evidence. She turned to the waitress. "You can clear the table now. Thanks for waiting."

Dana gathered her papers and put them back into the sheath, then dumped the file into her tote.

Laney stepped over to her, the filled evidence bag in hand. "Thanks."

"You're welcome."

"Why did you do this?" Laney's sunglasses rested parked atop her head.

"I couldn't help but overhear your conversation. An opportunity arose, so..."

"You seized it. I see." Laney faced Dana squarely. "You're convinced Vinn is innocent."

"I know he is innocent, Laney. Just as I know, until the real murderer is behind bars, I have three hundred other kids still in jeopardy."

"How do you know Vinn's confession isn't real? You're a school principal and a psychologist, for heaven's sake. You know better than most that given the right circumstances anyone can kill."

"Yes, of course, I do. But Vinn didn't. For those same reasons, I know that, too," Dana said quietly. "I just can't prove it."

"I hear an unspoken *yet* on the end of that remark." Compassion crossed Laney's face and settled into a frown. "Dana, you want to protect your students. I get that. I want to protect them, too."

"Of course, you do."

"Well, then. Let's do what we do best. You are the pro at the school, so I won't try to run it, and I'm the pro at police work, so don't you try to run my investigation, okay? Just do your job and let me do my job."

"Sharing a few notes, but I wouldn't dream of interfering."

Laney cleared her throat. "Course not." She backed up a step and checked her watch. "If I hurry, I can get this to the lab before the press conference."

"Don't forget girls' night out. Wednesday night."

"Seven o'clock. The Wine and Cheese House," Laney said. "I'll be there." She stopped and looked back. "Did you remind Julia?"

"She's on my list," Dana said. Julia Ford, a former investigative journalist who now wrote a weekly column for *The Firefly*, their community newspaper, which also ran in *The Sacramento Bee,* tended to forget. Actually, trying to forget is what had brought her to Shutter Lake—not that anyone knew it, and those who did, like Dana, were sworn to secrecy on the subject. "I told Ana, too," Dana added. Dr. Ana Perez ran the medical clinic. She was single like the rest of them and she might be able to offer valuable insight on Vinn.

"Sounds good," Laney said, then rushed out the door on her way to the lab.

Dana gathered the rest of her things. With luck, she could catch Thomas at his office. If anyone could get Chief McCabe to let her in to see Vinn, it'd be the mayor. One way or another, she had to get in to see Vinn.

If Thomas Jessup'd had half as much trouble calming the community as she'd had calming her staff, students and their parents, they both could use a soothing word, a quiet dinner and a stiff drink. Maybe two…

Want to keep reading? Order your copy of **so many secrets** by Vicki Hinze now!

THE BREAKDOWN NOVELS

(Best read in order.)

the dead girl by Debra Webb
so many secrets by Vicki Hinze
all the lies by Peggy Webb
what she knew by Regan Black

DON'T MISS

If you enjoyed *the dead girl,* please consider leaving a review so other reader's can find it, too.

Read Laney's short read: the story of the event that forever changed her life, *no looking back.*

ABOUT THE AUTHOR

DEBRA WEBB is the USA Today bestselling author of more than 150 novels, including reader favorites the Faces of Evil, the Colby Agency and the Shades of Death series. She is the recipient of the prestigious Romantic Times Career Achievement Award for Romantic Suspense as well as numerous Reviewers Choice Awards. In 2012 Debra was honored as the first recipient of the esteemed L. A. Banks Warrior Woman Award for her courage, strength, and grace in the face of adversity. Recently Debra was awarded the distinguished Centennial Award for having achieved publication of her 100th novel. With this award Debra joined the ranks of a handful of authors like Nora Roberts and Carole Mortimer.

With more than four million books sold in numerous languages and countries, Debra's love of storytelling goes back to her childhood when her mother bought her an old typewriter in a tag sale. Born in Alabama, Debra grew up on a farm and spent every available hour exploring the world around her and creating her stories. She wrote her first story at age nine and her first romance at thirteen. It wasn't until she spent three years working for the Commanding General of the US Army in Berlin behind the Iron Curtain and a five-year stint in NASA's Shuttle Program that she realized her true calling. A collision course between suspense and romance was set. Since then she has expanded her work into some of the darkest places the human psyche dares to go.

———

Follow Debra
Facebook | Twitter | BookBub | Instagram |

For more information on Debra and her books visit
www.debrawebb.com.

Made in the USA
San Bernardino,
CA